Becoming Cathy

A Novel By

Jim Malcolm

For Kate, in memory of a great vacation along the California coast.

"No one has ever died at San Simeon"
Tour Guide at Hearst Castle California
State Park, circa 1996

The stories in this book are works of fiction. The names, places, and characters are either invented or used fictitiously. Any resemblance to persons living or dead is purely coincidental.

Part 1

Surprise Party

Chapter 1
Bolton, Iowa
June 1957

After the plates of cold cuts and potato salad, after the cake, and after the gifts, my party separated into the men and the women. Such was the fate of all our family gatherings since Dad bought the thirteen-inch Magnavox TV in the walnut console for the living room. The men huddled close together, jockeying for the best view of the small and snowy picture, watching the sport *du jour* from the station in Cedar Rapids or, if the Gods of Reception were kind, from Des Moines. Since this was baseball season, they watched the Cubs lose to somebody at Wrigley Field and drank beer from long necked bottles.

The women, the superior sex, roosted on the front porch. Grandma, her bony shoulders covered by a thin shawl, rocked to-and-fro in the rocker kept there just for her. Great-Aunt Martha, Grandma's sister, sat at attention in a straight-backed chair. She insisted the chair was good for her back although she never looked comfortable sitting in it. The next generation — Mom, Aunt Emma, and Aunt Peg — languished in Adirondacks chairs, fanning themselves with the cardboard fans that Mom had collected over the years from the Mahaska County Fair. Next to Mom, a large pitcher of lemonade bled condensation onto a snack table.

Despite being the guest of honor, I sat on a folding chair. The good chairs went strictly by seniority. The other girls — my cousins Sylvia and Mary Lou — sat on the porch floor. Sylvia, at twelve, truly still a kid, sat with her back to a post and her knees drawn up to her chest, the hem of her skirt pulled up past her knees. "I don't care," she said when her mother, Aunt Peg, chided her. "There's no boys out here and I'm cooler this way." The Aunts tut-tutted, but I thought it was hard to argue with her. It was stifling as only a Midwest summer afternoon could be.

Mary Lou, age sixteen, sat with her back against the house. "If this were the eighteenth century, you'd be covered from your chin to your toes," she said, Gothic Romances being Mary Lou's current passion.

I envied Sylvia's attitude and comfort, but as a woman of twenty-three and our family's first college graduate, I had to demonstrate my maturity despite the heat. I pulled my damp blouse away from the faux leather back of the wobbly chair and wished in vain for a breeze.

I wasn't prepared for what came next.

"Cathy dear, when you are in Los Angeles would you visit poor Edward's grave?" Grandma said in a wistful voice. She rocked slowly in her chair. "You have a Kodak, don't you? Take a picture of the stone for me."

"Since when has he been 'Poor Edward'?" My mother's voice had an edge to it. "I never heard a kind word about him since he left home and this is the first I remember you — or Dad — saying his name since he died."

"Who's Edward?" I asked.

Silence. I looked at Sylvia and Mary Lou. Their faces were blank. Edward was a mystery to our generation.

Great-Aunt Martha sighed. "Edward was our younger brother. Your Grandmother is the oldest. I'm three years younger. Edward is ... was seventeen years younger than me. I guess he was a mistake from the start."

Squeak went the loose floorboard under Grandma's rocking chair.

Grandma cleared her throat. "As the only son, Edward should have taken over the family farm equipment business. That's what he should have done. He worked for Dad — that's your Great-Grandpa girls — in the office. Then he went to Chicago, to the farm machinery show. That's where he met her."

The squeak from the board under Grandma's chair kicked up a notch. Sylvia, Mary Lou, and I stared at Grandma. As far as we knew, our family was devoid of scandal. Our lives were as boring as oatmeal. The biggest disgrace we knew of was when Uncle Emmett fell asleep at Sissy and Norman's wedding and punctuated Sissy's "I do" with a buzz saw snore. This totally unnerved poor Norman, who was already wound up pretty tight. He couldn't speak after that and nodded his assent to the vows.

Grandma rocked faster. "I told Dad that Edward shouldn't go alone. It's a big city, Chicago. He's only twenty-two. That's what I said. I know Mother agreed with me, but she would never contradict Dad. So Dad let him go and look what happened. He came back with her. Married to her. Knew her less than a week. A Chicago woman!"

She spat out the words "Chicago woman" as if she'd bitten off a piece of wormy apple.

"What's a Chicago woman?" Sylvia said.

"It's what people are going to call you if you don't keep your skirt down and your legs crossed," Aunt Peg said.

Squeak, squeak from Grandma's chair.

"Oh, she was a pretty thing," Mom said, the edge gone from her voice. "Blond. Lovely complexion. Fine bones. Real fine figure. She wore a red dress the day Edward brought her home. Can you believe that? A red dress."

Aunt Peg could never stand to let Mom have the last word. "She was too fast for Bolton. Even Cedar Rapids and Des Moines. Iowa bored her. She wanted excitement. She wanted to go to California." Aunt Peg paused. A little flash of realization showed on her face. "Just like you Cathy."

Grandma and Mom looked at Aunt Peg.

Grandma rocked, her jaw set. The board squeaked at an alarming rate.

Mom reached over and slowed the rocking

chair down. "Don't have a stroke. It was all a long time ago."

From inside the house, the men gave a cheer and the TV announcer's voice rose in excitement. Then the sound of a cigarette jingle filled the air with the announcer's baritone voice, "LSMFT-Lucky Strike Means Fine Tobacco".

Softly, I said, "What happened to them? Is she still living in California? Did they have any children?"

Grandma rocked at a slow, sad pace. "No. No children. Poor Rosalie — that was her name, Rosalie. Her eggs were spoilt. They would never hatch."

"She had several miscarriages," Mom said in the patient voice of one who is accustomed to translating between generations.

"Her egg basket went bad a few years after they moved away," Grandma went on, her voice melancholy. "She passed on, out there in California. No one with her, only Edward. We never knew if she had any kin."

Mom sighed. "Mother, it's 1957. Queen Victoria is dead. We call them ovaries now, just like the doctors do. She got cancer in her ovaries and died."

"Oh how sad," Mary Lou wailed. The story seemed to appeal to her Gothic sense of tragedy.

"What about Uncle Edward?" That sounded strange coming out of my mouth. Five minutes ago I didn't know I had a Great-Uncle Edward. I looked at Grandma for an answer. Tears streamed down her face. Aunt Martha stared into her lap, her lips trembled just a little.

I looked at Mom. "About three years after Rosalie died, he was found stabbed to death in a park near the train station in Glendale — near Los Angeles. The police said it was a robbery. The family scraped together money for the burial and a stone, but it was 1936, the Depression, so nobody could afford to go there. Nobody ever has." She didn't look at anybody, just slowly shook her head.

"It's so sad," Mary Lou wailed again, this time with tears.

Mary Lou's wail stopped Dad who was on his way to the kitchen, both hands full of empty long neck bottles. He looked at us through the screen door. "Why so sad?" he said.

Nobody answered.

Cathy's father knocked at the door of her bedroom. It was open, but this was his way of showing respect to the daughter he loved. There were a few items still on the bed — brushes, and combs mostly and the carry bag she always brought with her in the car when she was leaving. The rest of the luggage was stowed in the trunk. Almost packed. Almost gone.

"Nothing more for you to bring down Dad," she said. She saw that the determined look on his face did not hide the sadness in his eyes. "I'll come back to visit. You and Mom can come see me. February is much nicer in California than it is in Iowa."

"It's a long way," he said. "A long way to go for a job."

"A job, yes, and a career." She collected the combs and put them in the carry bag. "Are you disappointed I came home from college with a degree and not a husband?"

"No," he said. "A husband would have kept you back east. I was hoping you would come home and stay."

"I'll be working with a great art collection in California. William Randolph Hearst owned thousands of pieces of art and antiquities. There's no place in Iowa that even comes close. It will be so exciting. I'll be making good use of my Masters Degree in Fine Arts."

There was a pause, then he said, "We'll keep your room for you as long as we can."

She stared at him. "What do you mean?"

"Your big brother is gettin' really serious with Sally. I heard him tell Fred that he was going to sell the '32 Coupe and buy her a ring."

She smiled. "Wow, I didn't realize he was that serious, selling his Duce Coupe. Do you think they will move in here?"

It was his turn to smile. "Hell, I don't pay him enough money for them to live anywhere else. When there are babies, we may need this room for a nursery."

He handed her the check.

"What's this," she said and unfolded it. She arched her eyebrows just a bit. "I don't need this. I'll have a job."

"Take it. Put it in the bank. It will help me sleep better at night knowing you have it."

She kissed him on the cheek. "OK. Just for you. Thanks Dad." The check went into one of the myriad of compartments in her purse.

He watched her survey the room one last time, confident, competent, grown. She turned back to him.

"Time to go," she said

Part 2

The Past is Prologue

Chapter 2

Glendale, California
August 28, 1936

The private railroad car loomed on the track at Glendale's Southern Pacific station. Skittish as a church mouse in a speakeasy, Edward Brown stole a look around a column at the car and quickly pulled back. What was there to fear? He was expected, wasn't he? A ticket in his name had been waiting at the ticket window just as he had been told it would be.

A well-dressed, blond woman walked by, the brisk clickety-clack of her high-heels reverberated across the cavernous platform. A Negro Red Cap pushing a hand truck piled high with luggage followed close behind. She looked familiar. Edward slid around the column to watch her as she approached the private car.

"Vincent!" she said to a massive Negro dressed in a formal black jacket, black pants, and a white shirt with a high collar. A black satin stripe ran down the outside seam of his pants, matching the cuffs and lapels of the jacket. Studs and a black bow tie completed his livery.

"Miss Stanwyck, what a pleasure to see you again," Vincent's baritone voice rolled across the platform enveloping Edward like the fog rolling off the Pacific. The brightness of Vincent's smile cast shadows in the early evening gloom. The woman tilted her head just as she had done in the movie Baby Face. Baby Face had been the last movie Edward had seen with his wife Rosalie before her death.

Edward watched Barbara Stanwyck standing on tiptoes, balancing with her palms lightly against Vincent's chest. She kept the lit cigarette in its long holder expertly to one side. Vincent bent down to accept an air kiss on each cheek.

"Front." Vincent's voice boomed. A miniature version of Vincent scurried out of the shadows and stood at attention. "Take Miss Stanwyck's bags and be gentle with them," Vincent said, a Marine drill instructor barking orders to a grunt. While the miniature struggled with the suitcases, Vincent escorted Barbara Stanwyck, movie star and sex symbol, to the private car and offered his arm to her for support as she climbed the narrow metal steps.

Edward fled to the protection of the column. *There must be other accommodations for employees.* Still the ticket in his name was waiting for him and typed on it was "Mr. Hearst's Private Car." That's what they had told him would happen when he called to make an appointment to meet with his employer, William Randolph Hearst, multi-millionaire publisher, movie mogul, and art collector.

A couple approached followed by a pair of Red Caps toting luggage. Edward recognized Gary Cooper. "Mr. and Mrs. Cooper, what a pleasure," boomed Vincent. Edward listened again to the ritual of boarding Hearst's private car.

Edward ran his sweaty palms over his new brown suit. Actually, it was three years old, but it was the newest suit he owned and newly cleaned. Money for a new suit was hard to come by in 1936 even though Edward was employed. He settled his hat more firmly on his head. How old was that hat? He was procrastinating, he knew. Oh well, there was only one way to know if he was really invited. What was the worst that could happen? Rejection? Humiliation? Arrest? It didn't matter. He had to try.

Edward hefted his wretched suitcase and approached the formidable Vincent.

"May I help you sir?" said Vincent, voice flat, eyes narrowed.

"I've an appointment ... err ... expected by Mr. Hearst." Edward held out the ticket, any confidence he had mustered now gone. A clipboard appeared as if by magic in Vincent's hand. He slid the ticket down the list on the clipboard.

"Welcome, Mr. Brown." Vincent's voice had warmed. Not Barbara Stanwyck warm, but warmer. "Will this be your first visit to the Ranch?" Edward knew the Ranch was Hearst's nickname for La Cuesta Encantada — the Enchanted Hill — once the site where the Hearst family camped when he was a boy and now a vacation destination extraordinaire. The Ranch, also called Hearst's Castle, but not to his face, was an ever-changing architectural project that was still incomplete. Hearst's desire to tinker with the design and seemingly unlimited supply of money meant any part could be redesigned and rebuilt on a whim.

Edward nodded.

"I do hope you enjoy the weekend, Mr. Brown," Vincent said. Then his drill instructor voice boomed,

"Front!"

Edward surrendered his suitcase to a miniature Vincent and followed him to the private car.

Edward sat at a small, round table in the corner of the private railroad car feeling out of place as a riotous party bubbled around him. A cloud of cigarette and cigar smoke hung at face level making his eyes water. A thunder like rumble of voices assaulted his ears. Above the din of the voices, the jaunty tune from the upright piano accompanied the shrill voice of the woman who sat atop it. He nursed his second Ginger Ale, watery from the melted ice. The bartender had offered to mix any drink that Edward wanted, warning him that he should get one while he could since Hearst kept a tight lid on drinking at the Ranch. The rest of the crowd seemed well aware of this fact by the way they patronized the bar. Edward asked for Ginger Ale.

A lightly freckled, strawberry-blond woman wearing a black dress bumped against Edward's table as the train jolted. She steadied herself, not looking at him, but at the noisy crowd. Then she turned to Edward and said, "Are you somebody?"

Edward said, "No. I'm an employee of Mr.

Hearst and I'm going to meet ..." She turned to watch the crowd again.

She turned back. "I'm nobody too so we must be related. May I sit with you?"

Edward nodded. She put down her drink, something blue with a tiny umbrella in it, and moved her chair close to him so she could see the crowd, close enough that he smelled the faint scent of lilac perfume.

She is young, Edward thought, *and as beautiful as Rosalie was when we met and married in Chicago.* A familiar ache came over him.

Isn't it marvelous," she said tilting her head toward him, still facing the crowd. "So many famous movie stars."

Edward looked at her, saw the glow in her face and his ache intensified. "Yes," he said. "But I don't recognize very many of them."

She gave Edward a conspiratorial smile, "You should recognize the two men talking next to the piano. That's Clark Gable talking to Henry Fonda."

"Where, oh yes. I see."

"Now there," she said, "is Jimmy Stewart talking to that bald man, a director I think. I don't know his name. Oh, isn't that Gary Cooper. I think the woman with him is his wife."

"Yes, she is. I saw them board the train." The din of voices and the ache were not as bad now. Edward searched the crowd for a familiar face and spotted the woman he saw on the platform. "Isn't that Barbara Stanwyck?"

"Yep, you're right. Oh, do you see that group of men there? They're all standing around Jean Harlow."

A platinum blond in the midst of a group of men threw back her head and laughed. "Do you know why there are so many men around her?"

"Because she is so beautiful?"

"No silly, it's because Jean Harlow never wears any underwear."

"What? No."

She averted her eyes and let out a girlish titter. "I know. I'm embarrassed just saying it." Edward watched a rising tide of color that made her freckles disappear and left her ears scarlet.

"Once," she continued, embarrassed or not, "she came to dinner at the Ranch in a dress that showed just everything. Mr. Hearst told her to leave until she covered up. She went to her room and came back wearing a mink coat. She's more careful with what she wears now."

Edward raised his eyebrows and shook his head slowly. "And how do you know all this Miss Nobody?"

"Where are my manners?" She held out her hand. "I'm Pamela Hudson."

"Edward Brown." They shook hands. "So Miss Hudson, where do you get all this gossip?"

"Aunt Marion ... my aunt is Marion Davies. She is a good friend of Mr. Hearst. She writes to me all the time about the parties and guests Mr. Hearst has. Aunt Marion is an actress, but you probably already know that."

Only the most subsidized actress and the most famous paramour on the planet Edward would have said if he'd allowed himself. He didn't. Hearst had been good to him, allowing him the time off from his job to nurse his sick wife. This act of kindness, during the depth of the Depression, brought uncompromising devotion from Edward.

"Oh yes. I know," Edward said.

"I'm going to be an actress too. Living on a farm in Missouri was so dull. The boys in town had no ambition to be anything more than farmers like their fathers. I wrote Aunt Marion and sent her some pictures my girl friend Peggy took of me. I was afraid

17

that I was already too old since I'd turned 21. She wrote back with a ticket and told me to come and meet Mr. Hearst. She said I would need to take lessons for elocution — that's how to talk for the camera — and poise and all sorts of other things you can't learn back in Missouri." Her voice dropped to a conspiratorial whisper. "Lessons in acting sexy." Once again, she tittered and once again, her freckles submerged beneath the rising color.

"I'm sure you'll do well," Edward said meaning the elocution and poise, but he realized she might think he meant being sexy so he flushed also.

They sat in silence for a minute, then she spotted another celebrity and the stories started anew.

The train made its last stop in San Luis Obispo around midnight. Laughing and jostling, the people who were somebody mobbed the door trapping Edward and Pam behind their corner table. Once free, they joined the crowd on the chilly platform. The passengers were being efficiently hustled into a line of cars while a gaggle of men sorted luggage.

Finally, the last car filled. Pam and Edward stood on the platform with their bags. A nervous man in a felt hat approached them. "Are you guests of Mr. Hearst? Going to San Simeon?" Pam and Edward nodded. "I'm so sorry, but the last car had two flat tires. Can you believe two? If you can wait here just a few minutes, it will be right along." Then he left, driving Clark Gable and a red-haired woman into the night.

Silence settled around them. Pam shivered in her short-sleeved black dress. "It doesn't get this cold back home in Missouri this time of year."

"Here, put on my jacket." Edward put his suit jacket over her shoulders and she rewarded him with a grateful smile. They sat on a wooden bench to wait.

"You're not cold, are you?" Pam asked.

"Oh, not at all." Edward was still warm from the residual heat of the private car and the effect of her smile. Again, silence.

"Can I tell you a secret?" Pam said.

Edward nodded. She was staring at her hands clasped in her lap, so he said, "I'd like that."

"My name isn't Pamela Hudson."

"Oh?"

"No. It's really Becky Stafford. Not Rebecca, Becky."

"Oh," said Edward again.

"Aunt Marion said that Becky Stafford is too much like Barbara Stanwyck so I have to change it for the movies. Aunt Marion said, everybody changes their name for the movies. It's not much of a secret, but I wanted to tell you."

Edward looked at her wrapped in his jacket, shivering once again. "I think that they are both pretty names, although Becky suits you better."

She beamed. "Remember that you have to call me Pamela Hudson. My real name will be our secret."

"Yes," Edward agreed, "our secret."

The car came for Edward and Pamela in just a few minutes. The anemic heater in the 1934 Model A Ford and Edward's jacket warmed Pamela to the point that she fell asleep on Edward's shoulder. The trip, which was normally an hour and a few minutes from San Luis Obispo to the front steps at San Simeon, stretched to more than two hours when a recalcitrant zebra chose to face down the car on the entrance road. Hearst collected exotic animals. A number of species of wild herbivores were allowed to roam the grounds. Carnivores were kept in cages in a small zoo. "Animals have the right of way. Mr. Hearst's orders," the driver said by way of apology. Hearst loved his animals more than people it was said.

"Can't you blow the horn and scare it away?" Edward asked.

"Oh, no," the driver said. "That will work with some of the animals, but not this one. I tried it once and he kicked in the side of the door."

So they waited. Edward didn't mind. The pressure of Pam sleeping on his shoulder radiated warmth throughout his body.

The zebra finally tired of the game and the driver delivered his passengers at 2:30 A.M. By then, the lights that brightened the façade and gave the appearance of magical buildings set in a Greco-Roman town were off. All that could be seen now was their pale ghosts in the moonlight. Pamela gave Edward his coat, a yawn, and a sleepy wave and went to her room in the "Casa del Monte", the guesthouse so named because it faced the mountains.

Edward followed a steward up the steps of the "Casa del Mar", so named because it featured an exquisite view of the ocean, and into the guesthouse. The steward carried Edward's bag into a bedroom at the front of the house. A large set of windows in a sitting room at the rear caught Edward's eye and he walked back to take a better look. A nearly full moon was setting into the Pacific Ocean, its reflection dancing and sparkling on the waves. "Wow," Edward whispered.

A cloud of smoke crossed in front of the moon and its reflection. The red tip of a lit cigarette appeared above a high-backed chair that faced the windows and a familiar voice said, "Yeah, that's always my reaction." A tall man with a thin mustache, wearing only a white, sleeveless undershirt and striped boxer shorts stood up. "I'll bet this is your first time here, right?"

The tall man looked familiar. He'd been on the train. "You're Clark Gable," Edward blurted.

The man held out an imaginary mirror. His eyes opened wide and his jaw dropped. "By God, you're right." He turned toward Edward. "You have me at a disadvantage sir. You know who I am. May I ask who you are?"

Several seconds passed while Edward's exhausted brain processed the question. Finally, he said, "Edward Brown. I'm an employee of Mr. Hearst."

"Most pleased to meet you Mr. Edward Brown, employee of Mr. Hearst." He shook Edward's hand solemnly.

Chapter 3

Edward waited in a small lobby outside the Gothic Study in "La Casa Grande" as the main house was called. Hearst often worked in the study, usually late into the night. Edward sat, his back forced straight by the carved wood chair that reeked of antiquity and furniture polish. Truth be told, it was hard on his rear.

Rapid footsteps preceded the burly man who shot through the doorway from the Gothic Study. Edward recognized him from a picture. He was Joe Willicombe, Hearst's right hand man. Scowling, Willicombe said, "Who are you." It wasn't a question. It wasn't even a statement. It was an accusation.

"Edward Brown. I have an appointment with ..."

"No you're not."

"I most certainly am." Edward's voice trembled with equal parts of terror and anger. "I called and made an appointment to see Mr. Hearst."

"Bring him in Joe," came a voice from the study.

When Edward entered the study, Hearst — a big, tall man with a long face in a light suit, was standing over a table covered with papers. Next to him stood a tall, well-dressed man with round glasses, black hair shot through with gray, and a bulbous nose.

"Mr Brown?" Hearst said.

"Mr. Hearst," Edward's words tumbled out. "I work for you, for the Examiner. I'm not in the newspaper end of the business. I'm in Accounts Payable, Miscellaneous Expenses. I ..."

"Please sit down Mr. Brown." Hearst's voice was firm, not angry. Edward sat in a chair that appeared as old as the one in the alcove, but felt much more comfortable. "Now, please start over again, slowly," Hearst said leaning on the table.

"I work at the Examiner, in Accounts Payable. The Miscellaneous Expenses section. We do the small expenses like Expense Accounts, office supplies, and so on. Not big items like newsprint and ink. I've been there for six years. Mr. Abrams is my boss. I've noticed some ... ah ... irregularities a couple of months ago." Edward cleared his throat, cleared it again. Hearst stared, his eyes boring into Edward.

"I had to check on a voucher paid last year. When I went through the files, I found a voucher I'd approved, except that I hadn't. It was for $250. If I'd gotten it, I would have had to bring it to Mr. Abrams for approval. I can't approve an amount that high. I checked others. There were a number that I'd approved — but I hadn't — and I found some that Stanley Burns who works with me had approved. He couldn't do that either. I was afraid we would be blamed."

"Why didn't you go to Mr. Abrams?" Hearst said, his eyebrows raised.

"My signature on these approvals looks the same as the way Mr. Abrams writes my name. The same for Stanley Burns' signature. Stanley and I are the only workers in our section of Accounts Payable who approve vouchers. After we approve them, they go to Mr. Abrams. Vouchers larger than $100 go directly to Mr. Abrams for his approval. That's the procedure. I have a list of the vouchers that were ..." Edward held out a wrinkled piece of paper.

Hearst took the paper without looking at it. He seemed to ponder Edward's soul as he stared. "Mr. Lawrence is Mr. Abrams superior. Why didn't you go to him with your information?"

"Mr. Lawrence is in the hospital with mononucleosis. He may be in bed for another month."

Hearst looked to Willicombe who nodded almost imperceptibly.

"So," Hearst said, "you called my secretary and asked for an appointment to see me and here you are."

Willicombe said, "Mrs. Crowley took the week off to go to her sister's wedding. The other girls are covering." This statement had no meaning to Edward, but Hearst chuckled.

"Well, Mr. Brown, thank you for the story. Relax for a minute and I'll tell you a story of my own. I'm having a gathering this weekend for some of Miss Davies' movie friends. One of them is Mr. Edward Brown and his wife. Mr. Brown is a movie producer. His wife is pregnant. That's why I was surprised to see him — but not his wife — on the guest list. It seems that the secretary who does the invitations was out last week and you talked to a temporary secretary who didn't know Edward Brown, the producer, so you got an appointment to see me this weekend rather than during the week." Hearst smiled a guileless smile. "That's OK. It worked out."

Hearst sat down in a high-backed wooden chair that creaked alarmingly under his weight. "Now, you must have left work early on Friday to catch the train at Glendale, right?" Hearst eyed Edward, but the eye had a twinkle

"Yes, only an hour early. I'll make it up ..."

"Because," Hearst interrupted, "if you had stayed until 5 P.M., you might have noticed that Mr. Abrams had late visitors. My lawyer, Mr. Nyland," Hearst gave a nod towards the well-dressed man at the table, "and a man from my auditor gave Mr. Abrams notice that his fraud had been discovered and that he was fired. You were right, Mr. Brown, Mr. Abrams did try to implicate you and your co-worker. The Auditor wasn't fooled."

Hearst rose, walked to Edward, took his hand, and shook it. "Thank you for your concern and loyalty. I truly appreciate it."

Edward stammered. "Mr. Hearst, it's you ... your generosity ... toward me when my wife Rosalie was ill ... three years ago."

Hearst looked up at the ceiling for a moment. "Oh, yes, I remember. Terrible sickness. It was the least that I could do. It was a tragedy when she died."

"I don't know how ... I, we were so grateful for

27

the time we had. If I'd worked for anyone else ..."
Rosalie had been stricken in 1933, the worst year of
the Great Depression. The company, under Hearst's
orders, has let Edward take time off to care for her.
Edward remembered the sympathy card that he'd
received after her death. "Miss Davies and I are sorry
for your loss." It was signed William Randolph Hearst.
His neighbors said that a secretary probably sent it.
Back then, Edward thought the signature looked
genuine. Now he was sure.

Hearst gave Edward's hand one last shake and
he went back behind the table. "I'm pleased that you
are here as my guest this weekend. Enjoy yourself."

"I can't do that. I don't belong with your movie
guests. I planned on going home right after our
meeting."

Oh no," Hearst said. "Stay. Have you met any
of the guests?"

"I met Mr. Gable at Casa del Mar last night."

Hearst grimaced. "Was he, ah ... appropriately
dressed?"

Edward thought about their meeting and
Gable's easy acceptance. "He was dressed casually, I
would say."

Hearst laughed a deep and heartfelt belly

laugh. He looked at Willicombe who smiled. "Mr. Brown. You are a natural diplomat. Perhaps you should offer your services to the State Department."

Edward smiled. "I rode up from the station with Pamela Houston."

"Ah. Miss Davies' niece. Well you already know two of the guests and it's only breakfast time. Why not stay?"

"Thank you, Mr. Hearst. I will."

Edward left the Gothic Study feeling light-hearted and light-headed with relief. On the landing downstairs, there were two men talking. Edward recognized one of them from the train — no one that either Edward or Pamela knew — and the other was the steward who had directed Edward to his room.

"I'm sorry Mr. Whittingham," the steward said sounding sympathetic, but firm. "We have a full house. I don't have another room that I can give you. The South Celestial Bedroom is considered one of the nicest guest rooms on the Ranch."

"It's so high," the aggrieved guest all but wailed. "I have trouble with my knee and I'm afraid of heights. I couldn't sleep in there last night. I had to spend the night on a chair in the Game Room."

A thought came to Edward, a way to repay some of Hearst's kindness. "Pardon me for interrupting, but I could take your room — heights don't bother me — and you could have my room in the Casa del Mar. It's on the first floor and the house has a wonderful view of the ocean."

Fifteen minutes later, Edward's suitcase was in the South Celestial Bedroom. *A perfect solution*, thought Edward. *Both Whittingham and I are happy with the exchange and the situation was resolved without anyone being offended.*

Edward joined a subdued crowd in the Refractory, the medieval-style dining hall. After his meeting with Hearst, he realized that he was hungry. He'd skipped dinner last night to make the train and he'd met with Hearst early that morning. He filled his plate with sausage, eggs, and hash browns, then scanned the room looking for a place to eat. He spotted Pamela sitting alone. She gave him a coy smile and a little wave.

"How'd yer meetin wid da Chief go?" she said in a Hollywood imitation of a tough old newspaperman's voice."

"Oh, we had a good conversation. He insisted that I stay for the weekend."

She raised her eyebrows. "You were going to leave? My only friend?" Edward began to apologize when she giggled. "Acting. Just practicing. But I'm glad you're staying. I did mean that about you being my only friend."

After breakfast, a group of guests announced that they were going horseback riding.

"Oh, I'd love to try riding," Pam said. "Come with us."

Edward had extended himself as far as comfort allowed for one morning. "You go. I'll wait for you here."

Edward had not gotten enough sleep the previous night. He sat in a chair in the Morning Room and tried to read, but with a full belly and a short night's sleep, his eyes grew heavy.

"Stay out of my business Whittingham," a gruff voice jolted Edward awake. Whittingham and a man with a red, bulldog face stood in the doorway.

"Good morning to you as well Bruce," Whittingham said with more sarcasm than friendliness.

"Don't get between me and Hearst," the other man said with a voice like distant thunder. "I'm making this movie, not you."

"We'll have to see what Mr. Hearst decides, won't we. What a lovely day. I think I'll take a stroll around the grounds." Whittingham turned and walked down the hall. A door opened and closed. The other man stared, body stiff and quaking. Then he turned and left by another door.

Edward decided that being alone might not be best so he wandered to the Assembly Room, looking at the paintings and sculpture. Gary Cooper, his wife, and another woman sat at a card table just beyond a potted palm. Cooper called over to Edward asking him to join them for a game of bridge.

"Well, I'm a little rusty," Edward said. He hadn't played since Rosalie died.

"Well Little Rusty, I'm Gary Cooper and this is my wife Veronica. Louella Parsons is your partner."

"Call me Rocky," Veronica Cooper said as her husband dealt the cards. He announced that they would be playing for a dollar a point. Edward gulped audibly and the stakes were revised to grains of rice to be paid off at lunch from the loser's portion.

About an hour later, when Louella and Edward had forfeit their servings of rice (Louella said, "Not good for my figure anyway") and the game broke up, Pam came in from her ride.

"Hi," she said to Edward, lowering herself carefully into an overstuffed chair opposite him. She smiled a wry smile. "The cowboy said that I'm not a natural horsewoman. I bounce too much. Now my tush is sore."

Edward watched the freckles sink into the rising pink tide. "You blush beautifully," he said.

"Oh hush. Come on. Let's go for a walk around the grounds. I am a natural walker woman!"

They walked out into warm sunlight. La Casa Grande, which had loomed darkly over them a few hours earlier, now glowed in the sun like a fairy-tale castle. Edward pointed out his new room to Pam and explained the swap.

"You sly fox," she said giving him a playful punch on the shoulder. "You must have a grand view."

"Actually it's scary. I only looked out once, then I closed the drapes." They both giggled.

They wandered through formal gardens and across wide patios. Lush, vibrant plants and a myriad of statuary surrounded them. Edward tried to steer them away from the nudes. Pam acted blasé, but was occasionally betrayed by the pink of her ears.

They followed the sound of water to a patio surrounded by marble columns. There, with a tumbling fall of water over nymphs and statues of fish with water shooting out of their mouths was an enormous swimming pool of light blue water. A delicate mist rose from the surface.

"Golly," Pam said. "Gol-lee."

Edward stooped and put his hand in the water. "Golly indeed. It's heated." They stared, so it appeared to them, at the courtyard of a Greek temple.

A chilly sea breeze from the cool Pacific broke their reverie. Pam moved closer to Edward, arms folded over her chest. "Hey. Aunt Marion said that there's an indoor pool too. Let's see if we can find it."

They explored. Leaning over a railing, they watched a herd of zebras grazing in a field. A change in the wind brought the growl of a big cat. Hearst kept lions and a tiger, in cages, it was said. Still, the sound was unnerving. They walked briskly in the opposite direction.

At the tennis court, they watched Jimmy Stewart and Irene Dunne batting the ball back and forth. The players stopped to chat with their spectators and told them the indoor pool, called the Roman Pool, was under their feet. "Go past that end of the court." Stewart said pointing. "The ground goes downhill. Take the steps down and you'll see the door."

Edward pulled open the door, then stood back to let Pam enter.

"Oh!" she exclaimed. Edward's heart leaped to his throat. What had startled her so? He rushed in stopping short next to her.

Bold shafts of light shone through the tall windows. Where the light dashed against the wall, brilliant gold, soft browns, and vibrant blues reflected off the intricate tiled mosaic of the wall. Further down, below an edge with a blue and gold repeating pattern, the pale reflection of the wall disappeared into the depths of a clear pool. Around the walls of the vast, grotto-like space, marble statues and alabaster globed lamps stood silent guard.

Pam, using her hand to shade her eyes, slowly moved her head up and down and from side to side, taking in the whole scene. Low and dreamy she said, "It's much too bright now, but I bet that this is so-o-o romantic at night." Edward nodded in agreement.

Lunch was an informal affair as Edward had heard it would be. He sat, so one of the waiters had informed him, in the "Hot Seat". "Don't be concerned,

Sir," the waiter smiled. "It's called the Hot Seat because it is nearest to the fireplace. When the fire is lit, it can be uncomfortable. But the weather is warm enough that we won't be lighting the fire this weekend."

Edward, looking up from his seat at the long table in the Refractory, noticed far above a line of heraldic flags on short staffs hanging on each wall just below the 27-foot high ceiling. Ancient wood taken from the choir lofts of medieval churches paneled the walls. Hearst, claiming he served simple meals reminiscent of the days when his family camped on this very hill, had ketchup bottles and paper napkins placed on the table.

Edward sat between Pam and Louella Parsons. Louella, recognizing Edward from the morning's bridge game, pointedly ignored him and turned her attention to David Niven who sat on her other side. Arthur Whittingham, the man Edward had exchanged rooms with, sat on the other side of Pam. "Thank you again," Arthur said. "You can't believe how much the height of that room affects me." Arthur Whittingham, it turned out, was a movie producer who had collaborated with Hearst on a couple of the movies Marion Davies had starred in. He was here to discuss another movie for Marion.

The lunch — salad, roast duck, green beans with pine nuts, and more — was hardly picnic fare. The conversation was lively, the cavernous room echoing with the timbre of many voices and no small amount of laughter. Arthur fed Pam a constant supply of movie gossip that she absorbed with rapt attention. When Arthur learned that Edward was an accountant, he said, "We could use more of your kind in the movie business. The people we have now only know how to spend, not how to account for it."

As dessert was served, the woman on Whittingham's other side — probably an actress since she looked a little familiar to Edward — took up his attention. Pam leaned over and said in a conspiratorial whisper, "Arthur is sweet on Barbara Stanwyck. See her sitting over there on the left? He keeps looking at her and when she got up between the salad and main courses, he stopped talking in mid-sentence to watch her." Pam giggled and Edward rolled his eyes. Middle-aged puppy love.

Hearst stood up, held up his hand for silence. "Everyone," he said in a squeaky voice that was much different from his voice earlier that morning. Edward knew that Hearst was not at ease speaking out in a crowd, even one of invited guests in his own dining room. It was a marvel that he spoke before political rallies and conventions when he ran for governor and congressman from New York back in the days of his Presidential aspirations.

"I hope everyone enjoyed lunch." A smattering of "hear, hear" and "thank you" were uttered. "For this evening's entertainment, Marion has asked for a costume ball. The theme will be "The Wild, Wild West." I know that none of you came with costumes since even I didn't know about this until this morning." He gave Marion Davies a stern look. She smiled and blew him a kiss. "However, I have a friend at MGM ..." He pointed at the rotund and bespectacled Louis B. Mayer who gave him a big 'say cheese' smile. "... who sent over costumes from the wardrobe department along with wardrobe staff to help us with them." There were cheers, applause, and a couple of loud whistles.

Hearst, smiling, held up his hands for quiet. "Yes, thank you Louis. Enjoy your dessert and coffee. I will see you all back here, in costume, at 8:30. Marion and I are going to choose our costumes now. Since I'm paying for the party, I get first pick." Loud laughter rang out. Apparently, if you were William Randolph Hearst, your jokes didn't have to be good ones to get a good laugh.

"How will I know you when I see you in costume?" asked Pam.

"Look for a cowboy. They'll probably have a cowboy costume that I can fit into."

"How about me? Aren't you going to ask me what kind of costume I'll be wearing?" Pam asked in a voice that was almost hurt.

Edward felt daring. "Don't worry. I'll recognize you even in costume."

Chapter 4

Edward entered the room, a Colt single-action revolver — the legendary Peacemaker that tamed the Wild West — slung on his hip. He wore his hat low to shade his eyes from the sun. Of course, there wasn't any sun. It had set a while ago. And it wasn't a ten-gallon hat. More of a five-gallon hat. The bigger hats didn't fit and the wardrobe man said that a big hat would get in the way when he was dancing. Dancing? Would he actually try dancing? With Pam? What an exciting prospect.

The band played to a room that was crowded and noisy. Whoever said Hollywood people always arrived late to a party didn't attend Hearst's parties at San Simeon. Edward searched the room for Pam. Even without masks, the costumes changed people enough that they weren't easily recognizable. Then he saw her, dressed like an Indian squaw in a buckskin dress and a black wig with pigtails that hung down her back. She was talking with an Indian Chief and a saloon girl — Hearst and Marion Davies. Just as he wondered if he should go over to them, she saw him and waved for him to join them.

"Howdy Cowboy," she said in a fair imitation of a sultry Mae West. "I'll show you my tepee if you promise to behave." She waggled a pigtail at him.

"Practice acting again?" asked Edward with a chuckle.

"B-B-Better watch out with that line here. Too m-m-many of these guys are looking to do more than pull your pigtails," Marion Davies said.

Edward had heard that Marion Davies stuttered. It was common knowledge within the Hearst Organization.

"That's true," Hearst said. "I'm going to deputize Mr. Brown here as your protector. Now you're Sheriff Brown. With his mean look and shiny six-shooter, you'll be in good hands young lady. You kids enjoy the party." Hearst and Davies moved on to greet other of their guests.

It had been some time since anyone had called Edward a kid, even in jest. Since Hearst had been born about the middle of the Civil War, that made him over 70, so perhaps to Hearst Edward was a kid.

"The Boss has given me an assignment. I guess you're stuck with me tonight," Edward said, wondering if he looked as pleased on the outside as he felt on the inside.

"Whoa, cowboy. Who's the little filly you've got there?" The voice sounded like a bad imitation of John Wayne. The speaker was thin, dressed as a Canadian Mountie, his wide-brimmed hat pulled low. He lifted his face and Edward could see it was Clark Gable.

"Mr. Gable. This is Pamela Houston. An actress. She just arrived from Missouri yesterday. And she is Marion Davies' niece."

Gable bowed, a slow and fluid motion, hat in hand as he swept it out in a flourish. "Welcome to our fantasy land, my dear. May all your dreams come true and all your nightmares be someone else's movie."

"Oh there you are," said a very curvy frontier woman in a calico dress and crinolines. "They're playing a tango. I want to dance!" She tugged on Gable's sleeve.

"Duty calls," Gable said to them putting his hat back on and followed the swishing petticoats onto the dance floor.

"Hello. Did you find the Roman Pool this afternoon?" Jimmy Stewart, dressed in an 19th Century Army officer's uniform and holding a plate of hors d'oeuvres asked.

"Oh yes," Pam said, "it's so beautiful." She gave Stewart a smile.

"And dangerous," Stewart said. "Be careful if you swim there. It's deep, ten feet most of the way around. I went off the board and tried to touch the bottom. Did too, but I was wondering if I was going to make it back up to the surface. The pressure popped my ears. I couldn't hear very well for the rest of the weekend. After that I decided I'd stick to the outside pool where there is usually someone around who will notice your floating body." They promised Stewart that they wouldn't swim in the Roman Pool alone.

The music changed. Somebody yelled "Lindy" and the flow of the party left Edward and Pam alone once more.

Edward let out a breath. "I'm just one of Mr. Hearst's employees. I came here to discuss some business. I didn't expect this."

"This is a big change from the cows and the chickens on the farm in Missouri for me as well."

They watched the dancers bounce. Then the

music changed.

"Waltz," Pam said. "Come on, let's dance."

Edward panicked. "I can't dance!"

She cocked her head. "The Boss gave you an order to protect me. I'm going to dance. Are you going to disobey the Boss?" She smiled. "Come on. I'll show you how." And she did. He stepped on her toes, but she said it didn't hurt. The hat kept them further apart than is usual for dancing. At first Edward was relieved. Later he wished that they could dance closer.

Near midnight, Pam tried to unsuccessfully stifle a yawn. "Sorry," she said. "The 5 A.M. wake up call is still in my blood. I'm having a lovely time, Edward, but I have to go to bed now or I'll fall asleep right here in your arms.

Fall asleep in my arms. What an exciting prospect. That's what he thought. What he said was, "Good night Pam. I had a lovely time."

Edward forced his weary body up the stairs to his room. The Celestial Bedroom was lovely, but steep and narrow stairs lead to the door. After Pam left, he had deflated like an old balloon. The wardrobe man had helped him out of his costume. Pam, presumably, was going through the same ritual in another part of the house suitably cordoned off for the ladies.

He saw it as soon as he entered his room. In the middle of the burgundy brocaded bed covering, a pale blue sheet of paper. "Meet me at the Roman Pool." The note was signed with a whimsical letter "B".

The letter "B"? Pam said her real name was Becky. It was their secret. She also said she wanted to see the Roman Pool at night. Edward put the letter in his jacket pocket and, light on his feet, scampered down the stairs and out the door.

He entered the Roman Pool, short of breath, long on anticipation. Eyes watched him. Edward looked both directions, and then set off to his right. Eyes followed. Not Pam's soft, blue, smiling eyes. Gray eyes. Hard eyes. Evil eyes. They watched as he came closer. Then, as Edward rounded a corner, an arm pushed a dagger forcibly into his chest. Edward's heart, which had been beating rapidly with expectation, tore and bled. The arm pushed Edward backward felling him face up onto the brilliant blue tiles, pulling out the dagger. The gray, hard eyes stared at Edward's ashen face.

"Damn!" said the voice of the gray, hard eyes.

There was a sound from the door. Without looking, the owner of the gray, hard eyes tiptoed to the far end of the pool and quietly went out an unseen door.

Raymond eased open the door to the Roman Pool so as to not disturb any of Mr. Hearst's guests who might be there. Standing in the doorway, he let the blue-gold glow of reflected light wash over him. The nearly imperceptible wavering of the surface of the pool, he knew, was not from wind nor from swimmers, but from the pumps that constantly circulated the heated water.

Raymond was a watchman as had his father been before him. He had the responsibility of checking the property at the end of the day. A few years ago, after his father had died, Raymond had been afraid of this new responsibility of checking the Roman Pool late at night, closing it up after all the guests had gone. The light and reflections seemed spooky, the emanations of the spirits of long-dead ancestors ... or worse. Soon, the beauty and solitude of the spot won him over. It was rarely occupied when he made his nocturnal visit. Once, the pool had not only been occupied, but he saw a man and a woman doing things which were not meant to be seen by others. The woman, mesmerizing in her nakedness, held his eyes until their ecstasy had played out and they staggered out of sight, holding on to each other for support and laughing over their shared indiscretion.

Tonight, a small sound when he opened the door stopped him from entering. He strained to hear, knowing if someone were using the pool, he should leave and come back after they were gone. Raymond heard nothing more except the gentlest of waves hitting the side of the pool and a faint hum of machinery. He eased the door closed behind him and walked around the pool.

He rounded a corner and stopped as if he'd hit a glass wall. "Jesus Christ," he said aloud and made the sign of the cross. In front of him was a man lying by the side of the pool. Seeing the red blossom on the front of his shirt, Raymond knew that he had not come across a lover in post-coital exhaustion nor a drunk who had fallen asleep. He turned and heedless of the noise, ran out the door.

They returned within minutes, Raymond, three other workers, Joe Willicombe, and John Nyland. They formed a solemn circle around the body, avoiding the pool of blood, not looking into the lifeless eyes. No one needed to check for a pulse.

Willicombe looked at the body lying next to the water, then at the workmen. All told, sixty, maybe seventy, years of service to Hearst. Years of mutual loyalty. Before he could speak, Hearst's lawyer, John Nyland, cleared his throat and said, "Mr. Hearst has troubles right now." The men made slow nods of agreement. Hearst's financial problems were no secret. "This," Nyland nodded at Edward's lifeless body, "will add to his troubles." It would also trigger Hearst's anxiety at any mention of death. No one knew how he would react to a death at San Simeon. He might leave the mountain retreat forever. He had other houses. Jobs, lifetime jobs would be lost, jobs that could not be replaced in the depths of the depression. Nyland gave them a final nod of benediction, then silently left padding on soft bedroom slippers.

Willicombe looked at Matt, the most senior of the employees gathered there. "It would be best if this went away." His eyes never left Matt's eyes. Matt nodded slowly.

The stars shone hard and bright in the sky over

San Simeon. The lights of two cars came on and the cars moved down from the Enchanted Hill. Tonight, a fog shrouded the bottom of the mountain. The buildings and gardens in the clear sky appeared to float on the fog like magic. As the cars disappeared into the fog, Raymond, in the back seat of the second car, turned and saw the moonlit outline of the main house sitting majestically above them.

The cars inched their way down the hill and through the gates that kept in the animals. Once on the main road, the lead car headed south, toward Los Angeles — the City of Angels. The second car rolled inexorably to the train station at San Luis Obispo. There it parked and waited for dawn. When the ticket booth opened, the driver got out and bought a ticket for Glendale. The sun rose higher, the day warmed. An hour later, the southbound train pulled into the station. Raymond, wearing a dead man's suit, hat pulled low over his face, carried a cheap suitcase onto the train.

Part 3

The Spirit of the Pool

Chapter 5

June 26, 1957

Standing on the platform of the train station at San Luis Obispo, California, I was almost at the end of my journey west. As I stood with my suitcases next to me, I wobbled a little, the result of two days on a swaying train exaggerated by high heels. The train ride had been, by turns, boring as we crossed the interminable plains, terrifying as we shot through the mountain passes and over the swaying bridges of the Rocky Mountains, and soothing as the train going north from Los Angeles hugged the coast. I'd traveled from Iowa to the East coast many times, but nothing I'd experienced previously compared to this trip.

I stood on the platform as the rest of the passengers headed for the exit. A man, elderly and thin, dressed in neatly pressed work clothes, approached and said softly, "Miss Fallon."

"You must be Mr. Rogers," I said and offered my hand. I'd been hired by the State of California to work at the soon to be opened San Simeon State Historical Monument. They'd been nice enough to search for lodging for me in Cambria, a town near the facility. I would be renting a room from Mr. and Mrs. Rogers.

He smiled a mouth full of crooked teeth stained by coffee and tobacco. His grip was firm, hands calloused. "Hope your trip wasn't too bad. Let me take your bags and we'll be off."

He grabbed my bags with more dexterity than I gave him credit for and led me to a shiny 1947 Ford. One of my brother's friends had one just like it. I settled back into the front seat, noting the condition. "The car looks almost new," I said.

"I take good care of it, wash and polish it a couple of times a month. We don't have the winters that you have in the Midwest, only more rain that usual. Your cold and snowy winters are hard on a car."

I recalled the icy winds that came out of Canada blowing snow and sleet across Iowa. Cinders or sand and more recently salt layered the slippery roads. After a few winters, rust pockmarked the cars and pieces dangled and fell off the vehicle. No snowy winters — California had potential as a place to live.

I wiggled in the seat. Although it wasn't worn, it did have a depression that was likely a match to the bottom of its usual occupant. I began to get a picture of Mrs. Rogers. Not of her face or even her body, but of her posterior. It was a bit broader than mine. I smiled as we set off heading north on the coast highway to Cambria.

We talked some on the way. "I hope the trip wasn't too hard," he said. "I remember going all the way to the east coast by train back in the Army. That was during the war, the First War. Cross-country on the train, then to France on a ship." He sighed. "It wasn't much fun, but I got back. When I came back, I was stationed in San Diego for a while. That's where I met Mabel so things worked out."

There were long silences since Mr. Rogers had to concentrate on driving. I was accustomed to straight Midwest roads. The curves of the highway as it hugged the coast unnerved me. Then there were the bridges. Always the ocean crashing ceaselessly onto the rocks. At last we got into town and pulled up in front of a wood-framed house, brightly painted with window boxes overflowing with flowers.

Mrs. Rogers was a short dumpling of a lady with, as predicted, a big bottom. She fussed over me for a minute or two, explained dinner would be at six o'clock, and suggested I must be tired so she would show me to my room. We went through the parlor where I spotted two large pictures hanging above the mantle, a Navy Nurse and an Army Officer.

"Oh, are they your children?" I said, then noticed the two gold stars on the wall above the pictures. Gold stars. Combat dead. It must have showed on my face.

"They joined after they got out of college. There were no other jobs, it being the depression. Kevin was in the infantry. He died on the beach at Normandy. Denise was a nurse in the Philippines when the war broke out." Her eyes gleamed. I thought of the stories of the Japanese overrunning the Philippines, the death march, and worse.

"I'm sorry," I said.

"Thank you. Was your father in the war?"

"Yes, Marine in the Pacific. He was wounded twice, but not badly enough to be sent home. He still gets Malaria attacks."

Mrs. Rogers made sympathetic noises as she lead me up the stairs and into a bedroom. It must

have been the daughter's room, I thought. There was
a four-poster bed with a pastel pink cover. I fell onto
the bed and slept.

Thursday. I started work next Monday. I
wanted to be sure I got to California in time so I'd
arrived on Wednesday. I'd decided today was my day
to explore Cambria. The Rogers house was two
blocks from the ocean. It could have been in Bolton,
Iowa, it being a four-square like my parents house.
Many of the houses in the neighborhood were the
same. There was the same hometown feel to
Cambria as well. I stopped at a diner for lunch.

"Are you visiting?" the waitress asked after she
brought me a club sandwich.

"I just arrived in Cambria. I'm starting work at
the Hearst mansion on Monday," I said hoping that
the rumble from my stomach wasn't obvious. "I'm
staying with the Rogers's on Maple Street for a while."

"Oh, Mabel and Albert," said the waitress who
didn't look old enough to be on a first name basis with
them. "They're sweet. They often take in new people
as boarders until they are established. It's a shame
about them."

I assumed that the shame comment applied to

the son and daughter who were killed during the war so I nodded. Somebody behind her called to the waitress.

"Be sure to see Moonstone Beach," the waitress said and went to her customer. I attended to the sandwich much to the relief of my stomach.

As I neared the beach, the houses became newer and some had the feel of only occasional use. The "beach" was as much pebbles as sand. The pebbles shone a multitude of colors and I did find a milky white stone with an opalescent sheen that must be a moonstone. I took off my shoes and walked into the water, then jumped back when the cold threatened to freeze my toes. I knew that California weather was warm and mild. I assumed that the ocean water would be as well. Surprise, it wasn't! Barefoot, I walked up the beach.

Mrs. Rogers was starting dinner when I got back.

"Let me help," I said. "I always help Mom when I'm home." That caught in my throat when I realized it would be a long time before I would be home again.

"Sure Cathy. Peel some potatoes and tell me about your day."

I talked and Mrs. Rogers listened, occasionally commenting.

"The Cambria Diner has been around forever. Abe Harris owns it. He's getting on in years. I don't know what's going to happen when he decides to sell." Mrs. Rogers, it seems, knew everyone in Cambria. Since the waitress at the diner knew her and her husband, maybe everybody knew everybody.

At dinner, I announced that I wanted to hike up to the town of San Simeon the next day. I planned to walk along the beach. My walk on Moonstone Beach today hadn't seemed hard.

Mr. Rogers' soupspoon stopped before making it to his mouth. "That's not a good idea. San Simeon is seven miles or so and the beach doesn't go all the way."

"Why not? San Simeon is on the coast, isn't it?"

"Oh it's the rocks dear," Mrs. Rogers said. "The hills come right down to the ocean. It's very pretty, but there isn't any beach for you to walk on."

"I'm going north tomorrow," Mr. Rogers said. He worked for the power company and they sent him every which way to look for problems. "If you want to get up early, I'll drop you off where the beach ends.

That's about four miles up. Then Saturday we can drive up to San Simeon. It's been a while since we've been there, hasn't it Mabel."

I can get up early when I need to so at 6:30 the next morning I was ready to leave with Mr. Rogers. Mrs. Rogers had made me a bag lunch and gave me a wide-brimmed hat to wear.

"The sun will be strong by noon. You don't want to get a sunburn for your first day at work." She sounded like my mother, but still she was right. I'd noticed a little color in my face from my walk around town.

I'd walked plenty in Boston and on hikes in New England, but my beach experience was limited to day trips to Cape Cod and, occasionally, Long Island. I'd forgotten that a step in the sand didn't go the same distance as a step on pavement so it took me all morning and much of the afternoon to hike the four miles back. Some of the time was spent talking with people on the beach ... the area was a popular place for people from Los Angeles — Angelenos they were called — to vacation or retire. The retirees in particular had a lot of time to talk. Aside from the rocks on the beach, I got one other surprise. Walking around an outcropping of rocks that was between me and the water, I heard a noise, like a grunt or maybe a groan. I thought that it might be somebody who had fallen on the rocks and was hurt, so I scrambled up to look. As I reached the top, something large and gray lifted its head, looked at me, and made the eerie noise again — only louder. I scrambled back down the rocks and sprinted a dozen yards down the beach.

Mr. and Mrs. Rogers chuckled when I told them. "I guess they don't have elephant seals in Iowa," Mr. Rogers said.

Saturday, as promised, we drove into San Simeon. We didn't walk around much since Mrs. Rogers wasn't up to it. That suited me fine since my calves ached from the walk on the beach. I found a taxicab company — Pat's Taxi — and arranged for him to pick me up Monday morning. We drove past the entrance to Hearst's Castle as it was commonly called. Mr. Rogers stopped by a field.

"Notice anything about those animals in the field."

A herd of horses grazed in the tall grass. Some were white. No, not quite white.

"Are those zebras?" I said.

"Yep. The zebras and some buffalo are the last

of Hearst's wild animals. The dangerous and strange ones were donated to zoos, but the buffalo and zebras stayed."

I hadn't even started working yet and already it was an adventure.

Chapter 6

My employment had the feel of being on probation. I worked for the State of California, but from July through December, the Hearst Foundation funded my position. Hearst's property and buildings at San Simeon were to be donated to the State on January 1st of 1958. The Hearst Foundation and the State were busily dotting all the i's and crossing all the t's to make the scheduled date. One of the Foundation's commitments was to inventory and assess the condition of all the artwork.

The expert contracted to examine the paintings had fallen seriously behind schedule. The Hearst Foundation, mindful of their commitment and watchful of their finances, searched for an assistant for the paintings expert. They inquired of their Boston, New York, and Philadelphia art contacts for recommendations for someone good and inexpensive. To their surprise, they received two strong endorsements for me. One was from Rutherford Gettens, a Conservator at Boston's Fogg Museum and also an instructor in the Radcliffe Graduate School of Fine Arts. The second was from Art Feldman, a partner in the Savoy Art Gallery and Auction in New York City.

I glanced up from the State Employment Application to catch Betty, the secretary, staring at me. I flushed at the idea of what she might be thinking. In Boston, almost all the women involved in the gallery art business were born to it, married into it, or slid under the covers with an artist or a gallery owner. None of these applied to me — especially the last. I turned down more advances than I could count including one so brazen, I slapped the cad hard enough to get a blood blister on my palm.

I would be working here the way that I worked in Boston — starting at the bottom with minimal pay. If I worked out, the State would keep me on after January first to provide continuity with managing the collection.

Otherwise ... don't give my room away yet Dad.

My boss, Dr. Thadeus Lowe the paintings

expert, appeared to be out of place and out of time. So far, I'd found a casual informality in both manner and dress in California. Not so with Dr. Lowe as he insisted on being called. On being introduced to me, he gave me a fish shake as we called it in Radcliffe, cold, limp, and a little slimy. "Pleased to meet you Miss Fallon." His voice was cold as apparently was Dr. Lowe since he wore a gray wool suit with a vest, a carefully knotted tie, and a matching handkerchief in the jacket pocket. He looked me over with barely concealed distaste. "We will go over your duties today. Tomorrow you should come dressed appropriately.

What could that mean? I thought as we got into his car, a nearly new Oldsmobile. I'd worn my hunter green dress with the matching purse and heels. My only jewelry, a pair of gold earnings, weren't very dangly. Maybe the shoes? Dr. Lowe was on the short side and in heels, I towered over him. In the car, he exchanged his glasses for a pair of sunglasses in a series of slow and excruciatingly precise steps. Then he took out a cigarette holder and lit up a Chesterfield flipping the match out the window with an odd wrist motion. Things clicked in my head. I'd been so worried about making a good impression that I'd missed the clues. So this is what the secretary, Betty, meant when she said I wouldn't have to worry about Dr. Lowe patting my bottom, that his wind blew in another direction. Dr. Lowe was a homosexual.

I knew that the first day of a new job would be filled with surprises, good and bad. Dr. Lowe was definitely unexpected. My workplace added to my disappointment. It was a warehouse in San Simeon, one of five that Hearst owned. Not even the Mission style warehouse that Julia Morgan, Hearst's architect for all his San Simeon projects, had designed. The Mission style warehouse, located near the dock, resembled a small-scale Alamo. This warehouse was a plain-Jane metal structure that had the charm of a soup can. Its contents consisted of a mish-mash — statuary, ceramics, furniture, disassembled panels from the walls and choir lofts of monasteries and churches, and paintings. All except the paintings had been identified by experts in the various fields, inventoried, and stacked neatly in the back part of the warehouse. Dr. Lowe was the expert contracted to do the paintings and like items — triptychs, frescoes, and so on. If it was paint or watercolor on a surface, it was his responsibility. And he was woefully behind schedule, so far behind they had hired me (over his objection it appeared) for fear the delay would affect the turnover to the state.

I couldn't decide if he disliked me personally, didn't want an assistant, or naturally exuded cold disdain.

He had rules. Do it my way or the highway kind of rules. Our job was to match invoices and storage records to the items stored. He took out a number of invoices and we roamed the uninventoried area of the warehouse locating the crated artwork. Once we located everything, we called the Castle and had a couple of men sent down to move the crates for us. Then we uncrated the paintings. ("Gloves, Miss Fallon, will protect those dainty hands, but I'm afraid the mortality rate for fingernails is quite high.") We examined the artwork to insure it matched the invoice, determined if it needed cleaning or conservation, and returned it to the crate — together, one item at a time. At the end of the day, the men from the Castle came back and moved the items to the inventoried area in the back of the warehouse.

Then there were the work hours. I must arrive at the warehouse by 9 A.M., no earlier. The day never went past 5 P.M. There would be no overtime, not even unpaid since Dr. Lowe must be present when I was there and he never worked past 5 P.M.

"Do you understand?" he said.

I seethed. I don't think I'd been on such a short leash since third grade. "I understand," I said.

A cab took me back to the Rogers' house. "How was your first day?" Mrs. Rogers ask politely.

"Confusing," I said which was true. Infuriating would have been a more honest answer. For a brief moment, I thought Dad might have his little girl back soon, but my Irish kicked in. I'd dealt with hardballs before in Boston. Dr. Lowe was difficult. I was tougher than that.

When I came home the next day, Mrs. Rogers said, "Oh my dear." I'd worn casual slacks and an old blouse, but they were never meant for the abuse received handling the crates.

After dinner, she came into my room carrying coveralls. "These belong to Albert. Try them on." She rolled up the legs and sleeves to fit me, then took them to sew. The rest of the week, I wore them, to the disgust of Dr. Lowe and the amusement of the men who came down from the Castle. On Saturday, I went into San Simeon and bought blue jeans and work shirts. I looked like the farm girls from high school, but they suited the job.

It was only Tuesday of my second week — day seven — and going back and forth to work by taxi was already a hassle. The mornings weren't a problem. Pat's Taxi picked me up at 8:30 and dropped me off at the warehouse. Convenient for both of us since that was the start of his day as well as mine. Going home was another matter. Quitting time was erratic, at Dr. Lowe's whim it seemed. If Pat had fare, I was out of luck. Dr. Lowe seemed annoyed that I needed to call for a ride. And he was annoyed that I had to wait for Pat, sometimes for quite a while if Pat was busy.

Two men from the Castle had just finished moving today's work from the workroom to the inventoried area of the warehouse when I called Pat's and listened to the phone ring and ring and ring. "Damn," I said and slammed the phone down.

"Problem?" said the younger of them.

"Oh, it's the taxi," I said trying not to pout. My father always teased me when I got angry because I made a pouty face that he found cute. "When he's out with a fare, nobody answers the phone. Now I'll have to wait around until five ... or later."

"I can take you home," he said quickly. "I go

past Maple Street on my way home."

I stared at him. "How do you know where I live?"

He took a step backward and wouldn't meet my eyes. "I heard them talking up at the Castle."

"They talk about me?"

"Well, yeah. They talk about everybody. And you're something new." He stopped talking and stared at the floor. *Good move*, I thought. *You've already put your foot well into your mouth.*

"Anyway," he said after a short silence, "I do go past Maple and I could take you home. I could pick you up in the morning as well. It's no bother. Really." He looked at his feet, kind of like a puppy dog that's been caught ripping up a pillow.

Well, why not. "OK," I said. "Take me home."

His name was Jack Goode and he'd lived in Cambria his whole life. He did go to UCLA for a semester, but he'd rather surf than study so he quit. He came back home and did odd jobs around town until he was hired at the Castle. All this I learned as I rode up to the Castle in the truck, squeezed between Jack Goode and Jack Andrews. Little Jack and Big Jack they were called. Jack Goode worked for Jack

Andrews so they were often seen together. From the Castle I called Pat and told him that I didn't need a ride home tonight. After stealing a look at Jack, I said that I wouldn't need a ride the next morning.

Jack drove me home in an old station wagon with wood paneled sides. I don't know much about cars, but this one just might be pre-war. It had a surfboard tied securely down to racks on the roof.

"Do you find many waves riding back and forth to work?" I asked.

"I check out the waves on my way home," he said.

"The beach is the opposite direction from Maple Street."

"I take the long way home. The less time I spend at home with my father telling me that I'm a bum because I don't want to go to college, the better off I am."

He dropped me off in front of the house. "I'll see you tomorrow morning," he said hopefully.

"I need to be at the warehouse at nine. Can you do that?"

"Oh yeah."

Mrs. Rogers met me at the door with a twinkle

in her eye. "Well, who was that young man?"

"Jack Goode. He works at the Castle."

"Oh, Edna Goode's boy. Richard Goode owns the Savings and Loan. Nice boy so I hear, but not a lick of ambition. He'd do nothing except surf if he could. His father won't let him stay in the house unless he has a job.

"Oh?" I said.

"Jack lived in that car for six weeks once. Mr. Goode got the police to arrest him on vagrancy and he spent the night in jail. One of Jack's friends gave him a job to get him out. Not a lick of ambition." Cambria was a small town. Mrs. Rogers seemed to know everyone's business.

She must have seen something in my face. "Don't worry dear, I don't talk about you. I keep my boarder's lives private as I would my children's. I talk to you so that you know who you are dealing with."

Jack picked me up the next morning on time, smiling and cheerful. He'd gone by the beach already. The water was calm. No waves. I called Pat later in the day and said that I'd made other arrangements to get to work.

Commuting with Jack worked out well. He was

always cheerful, especially in the evening. I needed his good cheer on many an evening when I could have killed Dr. Lowe. On Friday, he asked me if I wanted to go to a movie with him Saturday night. I agreed. We went out some more. I met his friends, people my age most of whom did not work at the Castle.

Then came the morning Jack didn't show up. I waited as long as I could, then called Pat for a ride. Pat was in a good humor. I wasn't.

"I'm not surprised Jack didn't get you this morning," he said. "I'd be more surprised if he did. Surfs up. He'll be at the beach until dark."

The men who came down from the Castle to move the morning's work for us confirmed Pat's diagnosis. "Jack doesn't come in when the surf's up. We've learned to expect that."

Well, I expected better. I told Pat to pick me up morning and evening until I told him otherwise and when I saw Jack, I told him much, much more. I'd worked for several weeks now so I had a little money saved. Adding that to what my father had given me "for things," I thought I had enough money for a little car of my own. Mr. Rogers took me to the Chevy dealer, a friend, and we looked at the selection of used cars. I settled on a Nash Rambler. It was just so small and cute, but more importantly, it was what I could afford.

Jack Goode was usually one of the men who came to the warehouse when we called and he worked hard at getting back into my good graces. As time passed, I warmed back up to him. He almost blew it when I showed him my car. I could see him clamp his face in place and say, "Nice little car. I can wash it for you." Oh, what the hell. There had to be some upside to being the pretty girl. He came over on Sunday and washed and polished until it gleamed. I suggested we do the same for his station wagon. He made a face. "The dirt's the only thing holding it together," he said.

I didn't say so, but I agreed.

Having my own car gave me a freedom I hadn't had before. I had use of a car at home, but I didn't have a job and my own money. At Radcliffe, I sometimes had a part-time job, but not a car. There was plenty to do in Boston without one. However, excursions to Newport, New York City, or Philadelphia were out of the realm of possibility.

Now that I had both, I felt giddy with the prospects. First, I had an obligation to my grandmother. I drove to San Luis Obispo and took the train into Los Angeles. Then, I took the trolley and bus until I found the cemetery where Uncle Edward was buried. The place was huge. Fortunately, Grandma, who had been Grandpa's bookkeeper and was good at keeping records, had the plot number and a map so I found the grave site without much trouble.

I looked at the simple stone. Rosalie Cooper Brown Born January 5, 1909 - Died May 13, 1933 and under that Edward Alexander Brown Born August 14, 1906 - Died August 30, 1936. I took a couple of pictures, close up of the stone and wider view of the setting in the open field of stones. In color.

It was still early. I'd planned on going to Chinatown for dinner. I hadn't had Chinese food since I'd left Boston. Iowa wasn't the place to go looking for Chinese and Cambria was strictly a meat and potatoes town. I'd heard of a gallery in LA which had a Rubens painting on display and from the map, I could see it was on the bus route between the cemetery and Chinatown.

I found the Ferus gallery easily. When I went in, a gallery employee asked if he could help. I told him my background and where I worked. He showed me where the painting was and told me to take as much time as I wanted to look at it.

There was a tall man there looking at the painting. He moved over for me. "I'm no expert on art, but she doesn't look 'Rubenesque' to me," he said.

I looked into the eyes of the woman in the painting. She wore a black dress with red and white trim on the sleeves, topped by a broad, black hat with white feathers. "This is a painting of Susanna Fourment, the sister of Rubens' second wife. He painted her as a gift, like taking a snapshot today. He never did another painting of her ... she wasn't his type. Now he did do many paintings of his wife. She was Rubenesque — and usually nude in his paintings.

"Well thanks for that information," he said, "because she looks like my sister. If I told my sister I saw a Rubens that looked like her, she would think I said she was fat. That's a sure way to spoil Sunday dinner with the family."

Just then a well-dressed, efficient looking woman came up to him and said, "Mr. Ferus will see you now."

He said, "Nice talking to you," and followed her into the back of the gallery.

Chapter 7

I sat in the shade of the elm tree eating lunch at the picnic table behind the warehouse. Mrs. Rogers wouldn't let me out of the house without a bag lunch. She made lunch for me and her husband each morning. So I was eating a tuna and cheese sandwich and reading a trashy novel. Peyton Place. Pretty steamy stuff. There had been some talk about Peyton Place among the undergrads at Radcliffe when the reviews in the Boston Globe came out. Only rumors and innuendo filtered up to the lofty levels of the Graduate School of Fine Arts where strictly classical smut was read. It was mentioned at the lunch table at Administration when I ate my lunch there two weeks ago. The girls had pooled their money and sent Marie Clarie's brother to a bookstore in San Luis Obispo to buy a copy. They took turns sneaking the book into the Ladies Room at work and reading a chapter at a time. Sometimes they came out red faced and breathless. Sometimes pale. None of them wanted to chance being caught with it at home so Marie Claire locked it in her desk every night.

The girls weren't surprised that I hadn't read it ... I was an intellectual. That may be true, but I had as many hormones as they did and the California sunshine brought them out. I suppose all the attention from Jack Goode didn't hurt either. He was cute in a boyish way. Whatever the reason, I'd bought a copy from the same bookstore in San Luis Obispo on one of my trips into Los Angeles. Well, the Kama Sutra was never like this. The Kama Sutra was explicit, Still, the language was so flowery and the positions so, so ... gymnastic that it was hard to image it was really real. Especially since the only actual sex I'd ever seen was between animals.

Midway through my freshman year in high school, I had just begun to acquire those physical feminine features that boys notice. One of my brother's more crass friends had noticed and made a remark to his buddies. My brother made a few comments to his friend and apparently to Mother because soon after I had my first bra and the birds and bees talk.

One Saturday a few weeks later Roger, a cad even as a high school freshman, invited a few of us girls and boys to go out with him and his father. Roger's mother had recently left his father and Roger, having declared them both beyond redemption. She took her three daughters with her back to her parent's home in Sioux City, South Dakota.

Roger's father owned a prize bull and was taking it out to stud at another farm. Four girls and four boys went along, crowded together in the back of the pickup truck lined with hay bales, bracing against each other to keep from being ejected as we bounded over the bumpy farm road. Behind us in the trailer, the irritated bull vented his rage.

Once at the farm, we lined up boy-girl-boy-girl at the fence and watched the cows being led into the barnyard. The bull entered and once he spotted the nervously waiting cows, his penis extended enormously — or so it seemed to me — and he began to methodically service the cows, not all of who seemed pleased with the process. Roger kept up a running and randy commentary on the action much to the delight of Annie, known as "Easy Annie" at school. Annie had been an early developer in the physical feminine features department and used her charms to make boy friends. The braying of the cows and the sheer physical strength of the bull impressed me.

I was somewhat shielded from Roger's commentary by Brian who stood next to me. A slight boy, he blanched at the sight of the bull and barely breathed, never speaking during the entire show.

My father was angry when he heard. He wanted to give Roger's father a piece of his mind. Mom hushed him. "All the farm girls she goes to high school with know what's going on. You don't want her to be ignorant, do you?"

My father said he would be more than happy to keep me ignorant. He spoke so softly that Mom and I ignored him. Mom did give me a little advice afterward. "Farm boys, in fact most boys think like the bull. Don't give them the opportunity to act like one." She didn't have to tell me twice. Her birds and bees talk had left out some of the finer details. After watching the bull at work, I was under the impression human sex was effected from behind and I wouldn't trust the boys in high school to find the right orifice in the heat of the moment. Fortunately, I learned the error in my understanding before I embarrassed myself at Radcliffe.

At the Freshman Dance, just after a slow waltz

I'd danced with Brian — the inept dancing with the terrified — Annie came off the dance floor. She and Roger had been doing something resembling a bump and grind. She grinned from ear to ear and said, "Wow, now that got my juices flowing." It became her favorite saying.

Some of the characters in Peyton Place were uncomfortably familiar. I could see a parallel with Betty Anderson and Easy Annie, as least up to a point. Betty dispensed her sexual favors willingly. Annie made the mistake of being a tease and it didn't end well. Perhaps that's what made me man shy, like Allison MacKenzie.

Maybe it was the perpetual California sunshine or the freedom of being on my own, but my juices were flowing as well. Once, before I bought my own car, Jack dropped me off and said he would be back to pick me up at 7:30 for a surprise. When I told Mrs. Rogers, she looked at the sky and said, "Oh, I bet I know what he has in mind. You'll enjoy it." Later, just before Jack arrived, she gave me a cloth bag. "Cookies and something to sit on."

Jack arrived and we drove out to the rocks at the water's edge. There were a number of his buddies and their girls along with other couples and families there already. Mrs. Rogers' cookies were a big hit with our little group and the thin cushion she'd put in the bag drew a few envious glances when I sat on it and protected my bottom from the rocks. We sat, Jack and I holding hands, watching the sun inch toward the horizon, then sink into the sea. It was, as Mrs. Rogers surmised, a perfect night with clear air and a calm ocean. When the last sliver of the sun slipped below the horizon, the whole crowd clapped and cheered. We went back to our cars then to Dave's Sweet Shoppe, the town soda fountain and talked and giggled for an hour until closing time. Jack dropped me off and snatched an awkward kiss. Mrs. Rogers was waiting behind the door to ask me how the evening went. When I got to my room, it took a while for me to fall asleep.

"'i ho lassie." Phoebe's greeting startled me. Phoebe, a perpetually cheerful British woman, was the oldest woman of the group in Administration. "Well, glad I found you out here. I'm loath to invade the domain of the bloody little troll." Phoebe wasn't much of a fan of Dr. Lowe. None of the girls were which struck me as telling. At Radcliffe, there were two professors which some of my classmates suspected were homosexual. They were polished and sophisticated and they gave as well as they took when it came to flirtation and suggestive banter with the students. Many of the girls fawned over them, probably because they were considered safe.

I hastily closed my book and shoved it under the lunch bag. I had my reputation as an intellectual to protect. "Hi Phoebe. What brings you down from the mountain?"

"I'm the bearer of glad tidings. We just got word we can have one last campout at the castle."

"Campout? Like a slumber party?"

"Better," she grinned. "There's food and boys.

"Not to worry," she continued probably in response to the look on my face. The Hearst Foundation hadn't impressed me as being a supporter of coed slumber parties. "It's not as naughty as it sounds. We go up on Friday after work. We set up grills and cook out. After dinner, some of us go into the Roman Pool for a swim — there are change rooms for getting into your swimsuit — and after a swim, outside for a big bonfire. We stay up outrageously late and sleep on the tennis court — girls on one side of the net and boys on the other side.

"Oh," I said trying to decide what my mother would say. She was a thousand miles away, why was she in my head.

"This will be the fourth campout and probably the last. We will be open to the public soon." Phoebe waited for me to respond. "If you need, I'll talk to your mother and tell her it's OK. But you will have to talk to mine." She gave me an exaggerated wink.

The wink got me. I giggled like a little girl. "OK. I'll be there."

Phoebe said, "'ow's the book? A little spicy?

I grimaced. "So far, it's a lot like small town Iowa."

She nodded. "It reminded me of my Yorkshire village. So who are you? Allison I bet. The intellectual who doesn't think much about boys."

I sighed. "Yes and no. I kept away from the boys, but not for Allison's reasons."

Phoebe leaned toward me. "I feel a sad story coming on. Got your 'eart broken did ya?"

I shook my head. "We had a girl in the freshman class, Annie Adams. All the guys called her Easy Annie."

"Ah, your own little Betty Anderson. Easy to share her charms."

"Not quite. Annie talked a good time, but she was all talk. Easy Annie became Teasey Annie. One night she went out with two senior football players and a six-pack of beer. Annie didn't drink, but the boys got drunk, beat her up, and raped her. She got pregnant and left the state. She never came back."

"Oh dear. What happened to the boys."

"Nothing official. Their fathers paid off Annie's parents. After the boys graduated high school, the draft board sent them induction notices. No college deferments for them. I heard that one man from the draft board told them that if they got the opportunity to fall on a grenade, take it. That's the only way anyone in town would ever say their name again without a curse attached."

"Small town justice," Phoebe said. She got up to leave.

"Don't tell the girls," I said.

"Oh, I wouldn't do that. If I told what I hear, you young ladies wouldn't come to me with your problems."

Chapter 8

The letter from Mom bothered me. She thanked me for taking the pictures of Uncle Edward's stone and sending them. Then she said the pictures seemed to upset Grandma, made her weepy and sad. She will get over it, Mom wrote, but I was unhappy my errand had caused so much distress at home. I wondered if I could find out more about Edward's murder. Maybe it would set my mind more at ease. Maybe it would help Grandma.

I started in the library in San Luis Obispo. Using the date on the headstone, I checked the old newspapers until I found Edward's obituary.

Edward Alexander Brown

Mr. Edward Alexander Brown of Los Angeles died suddenly on Sunday August 30. He was 30 years old. Mr. Brown had been employed at the Los Angeles Examiner, a Hearst Newspaper, as an accountant. He moved to Los Angeles in 1929 from Bolton, Iowa.

Mr. Brown is predeceased by his wife Rosalie.

The obituary went on to list his survivors and funeral information. Died suddenly. What a euphemism for being murdered. Still, obituaries usually didn't list the cause of death even when natural. Murder and suicide were never specified. It was just bad taste.

The paper containing the obituary was dated four days later than the murder. A story about the murder itself should be in an earlier paper. I found it in the morning edition of the paper dated three days earlier.

Man Murdered in Cerretos
Park

Mr. Edward Brown, 30, of Los Angeles was found dead of a knife wound in Cerretos Park near Union Station in Glendale at 10 P.M. yesterday evening. Mr. Brown had arrived earlier in the day by train from the north. His suitcase was found next to the body. Police say robbery was the motive. The victim's wallet was found nearby with the money missing.

Well, that was shorter than the obituary. Poor Uncle Edward.

The next Saturday, I went to Glendale. I'd

looked up the addresses of the police stations and found the one that was close to the train station. They would have been the ones who investigated. They'd have a file. When I entered the station, I saw an officer behind a grill talking on the phone.

"Can I help you miss?" he said when he had finished his phone conversation.

"My uncle was murdered in this area. I'm trying to find out about it if I can."

"What was the victim's name?"

"Edward Brown."

His brow furred briefly. "Doesn't sound familiar. When did the murder take place?"

"August of 1936."

"Were you even born in 1936? We have a strict rule against giving out information to people about crimes which occurred before they were born." He seemed to find himself very funny.

I flushed. "Well ... I ... I ..."

"Problem Sergeant?" Another uniformed police officer stepped behind the Sergeant. His uniform was perfectly pressed with extra braid on his shoulder.

"Lieutenant, this lady is looking for information about a murder from 1936."

The Lieutenant motioned me over to another

grill. "That is an old crime," he explained. "You won't find information about a crime that old at a local precinct. This precinct wasn't even here in 1936."

"What do I do?"

"Central files would have the case file. They are only open during the week. Finding a file that old might be a problem even for them. It would take time. You would need a good reason to see the file. I don't know if they would even show it to you. It's not usual." He shook his head.

Disappointed, I left.

Chapter 9

The next Saturday I went to LA with the girls to shop. Going to LA was becoming a habit. We had two definite objectives. First, I needed a bathing suit for the campout. I hadn't brought one with me from home because of the limited amount of clothing I could pack. Work clothes were a higher priority and the bathing suit I had, one I'd bought when a sophomore at Radcliffe didn't fit very well any longer. I'd put on a little weight, mostly in the hips and the chest. Moderately coquettish when new, now that my body had matured a bit, it was on the edge of indecent ... in Iowa.

April, who would be married next spring, was on a quest for the perfect nightgown for her wedding night. She was nearing the end of a yearlong journey to complete her trousseau, a task which started when Joe had surprised her with a proposal and a ring. Everyone who knew April was astonished since it can't be said that she gave him much encouragement. She was notoriously shy around boys and anything hinting at sex sent her into her shell. Thank you twelve-years of Catholic school education. Joe had known her since fifth grade, but hadn't gotten a kiss until their junior year of high school. Three years later, he rarely got as far as second base, but April confided to Clarissa she sometimes let him linger there before slapping his face. That was as good as telling us all. When she confessed to Father Antonio, he told her to pray to the Virgin Mary to resist further temptation. She only confessed once to Father Paul. Father Paul ranted incoherently, but April did recognize the word "harlot." Father Paul was not a popular confessor.

Marie Claire drove the six of us to San Luis Obispo in her father's station wagon. From there, we took the train to Union Station. We shared the railroad car with a family on a day trip and a few workers going in for some overtime.

"Here we are," said Marie Claire in front of a store called Ron's.

"This is a surfer store," I said.

"What better place to get a swim suit?" Marie Claire opened the door and I was swept in by the tide. The front of the store was given over to surf boards and paraphernalia. We worked our way past the boards awed by the shine of their finely finished and lacquered wood surfaces and the colorful trim. Swimsuits were in the back of the store. Since most surfers were men, the women's suits occupied only a small corner in the left rear. A bikini-clad mannequin hanging ten on a surfboard marked the display.

"How about this?" Marie Claire held up a string bikini on a hanger. "Black is good for all occasions" We'll all be wearing suits like this." The other girls smiled and nodded and some murmured agreement, but none matched the enthusiasm of Marie Claire's bold proclamation.

"A good fifty cents worth of dollar a yard material," I said, echoing my mother's reaction to seeing a bikini in Life magazine. I looked at the diminutive mannequin. My undersized one-piece had caused some comment at the pool in Iowa. This bikini would have brought the police.

"I'm sure you California girls can pull it off, but I'm just a simple farm girl from Iowa." I turned to the rack of one-piece suits without waiting for a reaction.

I should have left Ron's and shopped for a swim suit at Gaylord's Department Store, but they wheedled and cajoled until I tried on a couple. I

settled for a white one. The fabric was unfamiliar —
thin and form fitting. All the suits had the same type of
fabric so I decided it must be for surfing. Jack had
repeatedly offered to teach me to surf so this suit
could be an investment in the future.

Poor April was the next victim. She wanted to
buy the perfect nightgown for her wedding night at
Gaylord's. The girls steered her into Madam Rue, a
lingerie shop that tended toward the risqué. If April
and I had banded together, we would both have
gotten to Gaylord's, but she hadn't come to my aid so
I abandoned her. Poor April. Shame on me.

We descended on the nightgowns, a pack of
ravenous crows tearing through the corn patch.

"Too long."

"Too frumpy."

A hysterical outburst of giggling.

"How about this?" Betty held up a black strip of
cloth with a pair of triangles cut out of the chest and
filled in with a filmy gauze and a slit up the front that
would have gone past April's belly button. April
blanched.

"Too obscene," I said, "but now I know where
the fabric for that bikini came from."

"I like this," said April holding up a mass of pink fluff and ruffles that nearly hid her.

Betty rolled her eyes. "Joe will think your mother picked it out."

"I don't care. I'm going to try it on." April bravely walked into the dressing room.

She came out a minute later looking like a puff fish covered with pink ruffles from neck to ankles. "It's too much, isn't it?"

Marie Claire said kindly, "He'll never find you in there April."

"Here, try this," Betty said passing a peach colored nightgown with a more reasonable set of ruffles. April returned to the dressing room.

"I don't think so," she said when she came back out. The nightgown came down to her knees and showed off her lovely neck. A set of buttons ran down the front from her neck to just below her navel. I know it went below her navel because the fabric was so sheer her navel, along with her white bra and panties, were clearly visible.

"Oh, you can open the buttons for easy access," Betty said and unbuttoned the front exposing April's cleavage and beyond. Her undies stood out in even more prominent relief as her entire body went pink.

"And there's not too much fabric," Marie Claire said grabbing the hem and pulling it up to April's neck. "That's good since it's going to be up to here most of the night."

"Stop," April said with a quiet sob and pulled it down.

"Yes, stop," I said. I went to April and buttoned the front up to just above her bra, then reconsidered and undid the last button so that the strap between the cups was exposed. I straightened it. The fabric had enough body that nothing would pop out unexpectedly on her wedding night. I stepped back and looked her up and down. "Sew those buttons closed. When Joe sees you in this, he will know he is the luckiest man alive."

The girls nodded their assent. April smiled and blushed again. She was prepared — at least clothed — for her wedding night.

Chapter 10

Mrs. Rogers met me at the door when I got home from work. "A man called on the phone. He said he needed to talk to you."

"Not my father? Or brother?" I asked wondering if there had been a family problem.

"No. His name is Adam Spencer. He said you don't know him, but that it is important. He's coming here after dinner, about eight. Albert will be here just in case." Mr. Rogers was going to be my protector. He must be sixty if he's a day.

"Thank you," I said. "I'm sure it will be fine."

We were all in the front parlor when the knock came on the door. The Little Orphan Annie show had just finished on the radio. Mr. Rogers got up and went to the door. Mrs. Rogers, still working on the needlepoint she did while listening to the radio, gave me a look and then watched the hall mirror, which showed the front door in its reflection.

I heard murmurs of conversation and the words "Miss Fallon". Mr. Rogers came in with a tall man and said, "Miss Fallon, Cathy this is Mr. Adam Spencer."

The man from the gallery stood in the parlor, hat in hand.

"I believe we have met already at the Ferus Gallery," I said.

He smiled and shook his head. "Yes. Looking at the Rubens, what a coincidence."

"You had lunch together?" said Mrs. Rogers.

Adam Spencer looked confused.

"Rubens the painter, Mrs. Rogers, not Reuben the sandwich. I had some time between appointments in LA so I went to an art gallery. Mr. Spencer and I were admiring the same painting by Rubens."

"Oh," said Mrs. Rogers.

"I need to talk to Miss Fallon privately please," Spencer said. I nodded to the Rogers' and they left the room. Adam Spencer leaned back to check the hall to see if they were gone.

"They're in the kitchen I'm sure," I said. "What can I do for you Mr. Spencer?"

He reached into his inside jacket pocket and took out a leather case like the business card case that Dr. Lowe had. He put a finger to his lips, a request for silence, with one hand and flipped open the case with the other. There was a badge and an ID card. The ID read "Detective Sergeant Adam G. Spencer California State Police."

"I need to talk to you privately. Can you meet me for dinner tomorrow night at the Mountain Roost on Route 101, say at seven? I'm following up on a lead. You may be able to help, but everything must be kept in the strictest secrecy. Can you do that?"

I was a little dizzy from the rapid change of events. I nodded.

He gave me a business card from the leather case. "If you need to get in touch with me, call this number. It's the main number for the California State Police office where I work. They will call my extension and if I don't answer, they will get a message to me. Remember, nobody can know. Now, when they ask you what I wanted, what will you say?" He indicated Mr. and Mrs. Rogers in the kitchen.

"I'll ... tell them that you wanted more information about the Rubens."

He nodded. "That's pretty good." He said his good byes and I walked him to the door.

I may not know much about the police, but I do know that meeting a detective for dinner doesn't sound like standard operating procedure. The next day, I ransacked my room for nickels, dimes, and quarters before going to work. About ten-thirty, I told Dr. Lowe I was going for coffee — something that I sometimes did — and went across the street into the diner. There I slipped into the phone booth and called the number on the card.

"California State Police."

"Do you have a Detective Sergeant Adam Spencer there?"

"Yes, I'll put you through to him."

"No," I said hastily. "I'd like to talk to his superior."

I heard the sound of turning pages. "That is Captain Murphy. I'll connect you."

"Murphy," came the brusque response to the ring. He sounded nasal with none of the soothing Irish brogue of the Murphys of Bolton, Iowa.

I told him who I was and described the strange meeting with Detective Spencer the previous evening.

"Detective Spencer is on the Art Fraud unit. Actually, he is the Art Fraud unit in this part of the state. You may be able to help in our investigation.

He'll explain. Your help could be important."

I thanked Captain Murphy and hung up. I was going out to dinner tonight.

The Mountain Roost was nice, almost posh. My blue, polka-dot dress felt comfortable in the warm night air. Detective Spencer ordered a beer. I declined the offer of a glass of wine and we ordered dinner. "I wanted anyone who might see us together to think this was a date," he said. "The whole situation is sensitive. We don't want to spook anyone or create any publicity unless we find out something wrong is going on. You understand, right?"

"I will when you explain it all to me, Detective Spencer," I said as the entree was served.

He leaned over the table to get close to me. I instinctively leaned towards him. "Please. Our meeting must appear to be social even if this is the only time we meet. Call me Adam. And allow me to call you Cathy. No one can know I'm a policeman. OK?"

"OK," I replied and sat back.

Detective Spencer then explained his investigation. It was simple. Rumors had surfaced that someone was selling paintings stolen from the Hearst collection. He had been at the Ferus gallery talking to the owner who had a reliable source for these rumors.

"We just need you to keep your eyes open for anything that looks odd or out of place. Not even suspicious, just odd. We've tried to verify, very discretely, that some things may be missing, but everything's in place. Still, the rumors persist and from good sources."

"Have other galleries heard these stories?" I asked. Detective Spencer nodded. That would arouse alarm in the art gallery circles. Art dealers regarded art the way bankers regard money. Stolen art was bad. Once thefts became known, people became suspicious, reluctant to trust. This slowed down commerce and the art dealers stopped making money.

"Why not ask Dr. Lowe?" I said.

Spencer took a few seconds before answering. "Dr. Lowe can be difficult to work with, so I've been told. He may take our questions as an accusation or he may not help for fear it will come back on him. I understand he already has problems with the Hearst Foundation because he is so late. Being new, you are in a better position to help."

He paused again. "The Hearst Foundation and

certain people in the state government want this project to be a success. There are other people in the government who consider this project a dumb idea and would like a scandal so that they could derail it. That's why we need your discretion."

I wanted the project to succeed also. In her last letter, Mom wrote she was getting ready to send her winter coat out for its pre-season cleaning. Visions of a snowy Iowa winter sent a shiver down my spine. "I'll help any way I can."

A motion caught my eye. April and a man, probably her fiancé Joe, sat at a table for two on the other side of the room. April and I had been the victims of the girls in Administration on last weekend's shopping trip to LA. She was a sweetheart really. She befriended me in church soon after I arrived and I hadn't even remembered meeting her at the Castle that first day on the job.

April waved to me. I waved back and smiled.

"Who's that?" Spencer asked.

"April. She works at the Castle. I guess that is her fiancé Joe with her."

"And when she asks you who I am, what will you say?"

That stopped me short. I hadn't realized

helping would involve deception.

"You're my cousin from Los Angeles. I do ... did have an uncle who lived in Los Angeles."

"Good! You can think under pressure." He gave me a rueful smile. "Sorry to make you life so complicated, but it is important."

We finished dinner. Over coffee, a thought came to me. "Maybe you could do me a favor," I said.

He looked at me over his coffee cup. "I can't fix tickets, they are local government."

"No, it's not like that." I explained to him about Edward's murder and my experience at the police station. He wrote down Edward's name and the date and place of the murder.

"I can see why you got that reaction. They have enough murders to work on that are twenty minutes old. A twenty-year-old murder isn't even on their radar. I'll ask around and see what I can find out."

After dinner, we walked out to the parking lot. Then, under his breath he said, "Damn, Lowe's coming." He spun around in front of me and put his hand around my waist. "Kiss me," he hissed. He pulled me up to him, his lips on mine, his hat brim cutting into my forehead. He smelled of cigar smoke, sweat, and beer. His five o-clock shadow rubbed against my cheek. I got a glance of Dr. Lowe and then I closed my eyes. Spencer held me until his footsteps faded.

"Sorry," he said and released his grip on me. I pushed away from him and turned around — the parking lot was empty of people. "I don't think he noticed us ... or you."

"Next time you spring a kiss on a girl," I said, just a little angry, "shave first."

Two days later, Adam Spencer called me at home. "It's that Mr. Spencer again," Mrs. Rogers said when she called me to the phone.

"There is a retired detective, name of Johnnie Brady who is a walking encyclopedia of every unsolved murder in the LA area for the last thirty years. I talked to him and he remembers your uncle's murder. He says he will talk to you." Adam gave me a phone number. The next day I called and talked to his wife. She wasn't too happy about it, but Johnnie took the phone away from her and agreed to meet me on Sunday. He gave me his address.

Chapter 11

The early autumn sun stood high in the clear sky as our rag-tag caravan of cars wound its way up the mountain. We parked and unpacked our load — grills, charcoal, and food — onto the grass. Soon the air was ripe with aroma of char broiled meat. Burgers and hot dogs were consumed. The pitch and volume of the voices rose as they tumbled through the mountains. Sometimes the sharp call of a bird or the screech of an animal pierced the twilight followed by a girlish shriek, which in turn was followed by laughter.

The sun still shown as I followed a small crowd to a door located under the tennis courts into the Roman Pool. "Wow," I said as my eyes took in the sight.

"Ow, sorry," said April. She was right behind me and hadn't noticed that I'd stopped. "Pretty isn't it. It's even nicer when the sun goes down and all the light comes from the lamps." Around the perimeter of the pool, large globes cast a mellow illumination.

I changed into my suit and followed the voices to the shallow end of the pool. I was pleased with the suit. My skin had just a bit of color from the sun which contrasted nicely with the white of the fabric. The suit also had a blue band around the waist that I thought made it look modern.

About a dozen people were sitting on the side of the pool with their legs dangling in the water. None of the girls, I noted, wore a bikini. I sat with the group and put my feet in the water. Chills shot up my legs! The pool heater hadn't been on for more than a decade. No wonder there were so few people swimming.

Jack and some of the other guys horsed around in the water. In a couple of minutes Jack noticed me. "Come on in Cathy," he said, in a taunting, little-boy sort of way. "Not scared of the water, are you?" He splashed water my way. I splashed some back. He splashed more.

"OK, I'll show you," I said getting up and backing up to the wall. I ran across the narrow apron of tile that surrounded the pool, sailing through the air with my knees pulled up to my chest and my head down. I landed a near perfect cannonball a couple of feet from him dowsing him in a splendid geyser of water.

I came up in water just above my waist. Jack was shaking the water out of his face while the rest of the group applauded me. Jack stopped shaking. His smile slackened and his eyes widened. The guys who had been applauding went silent. I looked down. I expected my nipples to be hard in the cold water. I suspected that the hardness would show through the thin fabric of the swimsuit. And it did. I didn't expect to have the fabric of the suit turn translucent and show my dark areola.

I pushed a vicious wall of water at Jack filling his open mouth and stalked to the side of the pool. Behind me, Jack sputtered as the other guys cheered and jeered. At the edge of the pool, I stood in waist deep water with my arms folded across my chest and called out, "April. Get me my towel." She did. Fast. I folded the towel around my chest letting the long end drape into the water halfway down my thigh. I wasn't going to chance the bottom half of the suit being as see-through as the top. With as much dignity as I could muster, I walked to the shallow end and up the stairs.

Jack stood beside me and tried to apologize. I ignored him. I ignored them all. I was seething with anger and embarrassment, mostly embarrassment. I needed to burn it off. I needed to get away from them, especially Jack. "Allison, isn't there a diving board somewhere?" Allison made up pamphlets, which include floor plans for the upcoming opening to the public. She was the resident expert on the layout of the houses and outbuildings.

Allison squinted since she wasn't wearing her glasses giving her a Mr. McGoo look, pointed and said, "Yes. It's not a very high board."

I got up and gathered my towel chastely around me. Jack followed me until we went around the corner that cut us off from the view of the rest of the crowd. I whirled around causing him to stop short. "Go away," I said softly and slowly.

"You can't swim alone. It's not safe."

"Go Away." Still soft and slow, but with menace I hoped.

"But ..."

"I'm not giving you a private peep show. I want to be alone so I can dive so GO AWAY."

"It's really deep here."

"GO ..."

"OK, I'm going." He held up his hands palm out. Just before he rounded the corner, he looked back and said, "Be careful."

Jack had brought back all the embarrassment and anger though now it was tilted towards anger. He did that to me at times. I dropped my towel and mounted the board, trying to put it all out of my mind. Around me, the walls glowed from the colored tiles with gold in them. The bottom of the pool looked a million miles away. I took a breath and dove down aiming for the bottom.

I didn't make it. When I finally gave up the bottom seemed as far way as it had from the board. I pulled myself out of the pool and panted.

Damn, you dive like a girl I thought to myself echoing my brother's taunt about my baseball throwing ability. Back on the board, I breathed deeply for a minute and dove in again.

Same result, almost. Just before I turned towards the surface, I could see in the dim light that the bottom was noticeably closer.

I stood on the board a third time hyperventilating, breathing in and out rapidly until there was a little tingle in my fingertips and toes and I became light-headed. *Third time's a charm* I thought and dove, then kicked and stroked towards my goal. I touched bottom softly and turned, then with a powerful kick, I rushed upwards. Who dives like a girl I almost said aloud as I broke the surface. A minute later, I was sitting with my back against the cool tile wall watching the waves on the surface of the pool. The place was hypnotic. The tiles on the walls glowed, the voices of the rest of the gang drifted away, and the pool water was still.

Above the pool, light coalesced into a soft glowing ball. Below the ball, the water began to ripple — not ripples like a rock in a lake, but concentric circles of quivering water. I felt a chill. Every goose bump my body could muster rose up.

"Hello." The word formed around me.

"Hello yourself," I whispered. Something about the scene made me fear my voice, if too loud, could destroy it.

"It's been a long time since anyone stopped here. What's your name?"

"Cathy Fallon. What's yours?"

The glow increased for a moment and the ripples became more agitated, then they waned. Was my question impertinent? The glow and ripples came back to normal. "I don't know," it said.

"Oh, that's sad. Everyone should have a name." We both fell silent. It occurred to me that perhaps I should feel frightened, but I wasn't. The scene was so surreal I didn't feel threatened, but I did feel at a loss for something to say. A number of girls at Radcliffe had gone to finishing school to learn the appropriate social graces. I wondered if conversing with a spirit had come up in any of their classes.

"What do you remember?" I asked. "Maybe we can figure it out." It was worth a try.

The light cycled through several shades of red before coming back to its normal yellow glow. I felt a sigh. "It's all a jumble. I traveled on a train. I wore a suit. Then I was wearing a cowboy hat, but I wasn't riding a horse. She rode a horse, but not while I wore the cowboy hat. She wasn't wearing a cowboy hat either. She was dressed as an Indian squaw."

"She?"

The light cycled through more colors faster than I could follow. "A lady. Pretty. Young. Like you. She talked to me. She said, 'The boss said to protect me and you wouldn't want to disobey the boss.' She was nice."

The glow dimmed. "I'm tired. I have to go now. Please come back." Then it was gone.

Chapter 12

I was getting good at going into Los Angeles. I took a taxi to the Brady house since it lay well off the trolley and bus routes. His wife met me at the door and stepped outside. "Don't get him all worked up," she said. "These old cases eat at him. They gave him a heart attack. That's why he retired. Otherwise he'd still be at his desk reading old case files."

Johnnie Brady, short, barrel chested, and gray haired, took me into his den and pointedly closed the door in his wife's face. He looked me up and down and said, "What do you know?"

I told him what my grandmother had told me and showed him the receipts for the grave and the stone and the map of the cemetery.

He unlocked a file cabinet and took a file from the top drawer. "This was the second murder I investigated after I joined Homicide," he said. "Officially, your uncle was killed during the commission of a robbery. It wasn't that unusual at that time. Money was hard to come by. People were desperate."

His voice sounded skeptical. "But you don't think so?"

"No. Three things bothered me. First, was the murder weapon, a knife with a curved blade." He took a Coroner's Report out of the file and pointed to a paragraph. "In thirty years, I have yet to see another murder with a knife with a curved blade."

"Second, the body had been undressed and redressed."

"How do you know?"

He showed me a photograph of the body. "Look closely. What do you see?"

I looked. A man lay on the ground face down. Nothing looked amiss to me.

"Look at his shoes."

I looked. "They're on the wrong feet!"

He smiled in triumph. "Third, the time line is screwy. He reportedly left San Luis Obispo by train at 6:12 A.M., but the body wasn't found until 10:30 P.M. The coroner says that when it was found, he'd been dead about twenty-four hours. Something was screwy about the whole case."

"And there's the note." He took a copy of a note out of the file. "Meet me at the Roman Pool. B" The script could have been feminine, but it was hard to be sure.

"The Roman Pool? That's at San Simeon. What did this have to do with Hearst?"

"Your uncle had been to see Hearst. He left unexpectedly Sunday morning, or so that's the story. Hearst was off limits. End of investigation."

The next Wednesday, while doing an errand for Dr. Lowe, I saw Gwen Sanchez, the San Simeon historian that worked for the Hearst Foundation. After we exchanged greetings, I said, "Gwen, has anyone ever died at San Simeon?"

"Oh, no," she said, but she gave me a guarded look and her body language changed. "Why do you ask?"

I hadn't expected that question. The apparition in the pool seemed to me to be a ghost. To get a ghost, there must be a death. The conclusion was logical although I didn't want to tell Gwen. I thought about how to answer. I must have hesitated too long.

She said, "You've seen the ghost in the Roman Pool?"

"Huh?"

"There have been stories of a ghost in the Roman Pool since the late 1930's. He shows up about once a year. A quiet type, no moans or boos or anything. I think it's probably just the reflections down there."

"You're probably right," I said. The best thing to do was to agree and drop the subject.

"There was one guest who left unexpectedly on Sunday morning and was found dead that night." The historian in her seemed to take over. She had information and just had to tell.

"That sounds odd. Why did he leave?"

"Nobody saw him leave. Nobody knows." She shook her head. "I do have the guest list for that weekend so we can figure out the name. Stop by my office the next time you're at the Administration Building."

The next day as we left the warehouse, Dr. Lowe told me not to come in until noon the following day. "You will just be waiting outside for me to open the door if you do," he said and slipped into his car not waiting for a reply. OK. I could deal with that. The next morning I drove instead to the Administration

Building and stopped at Gwen's office.

"Hi," Gwen said. "Are you here for the list? I typed up a copy for you." She plucked a sheet of paper from her desk. "This list has some corrections which makes it a little confusing, but I checked and this is the guy who was killed." She pointed to a line on the list. It had originally read: Mr. and Mrs. Edward Brown (Producer)Casa del Mar. However, the words "and Mrs." were crossed out. "Producer" was also crossed out and the word "Employee" penciled in. Lastly, a penciled in line with an arrowhead on each end ran from "South Celestial Bedroom" next to the name "Arthur Whitingham" to "Casa del Mar" next to the name "Edward Brown." The copy she had typed for me had the same penciled changes. "I think the lines with the double arrowheads indicate they swapped rooms."

"Are all the guest sheets like this?" I asked.

"We don't know. They were always discarded after the weekend was over. They kept this one because the police called and asked about him. The head steward used this copy so it has any last minute changes. That's also why it has the occupation. The steward needed to know who he was dealing with. It's odd that an employee came for the weekend. They usually came for the day during the week."

My heart was beating hard. "Are you sure that it was the same Edward Brown who was killed."

"Pretty sure. There was a note in the file that the police had called to ask why he left unexpectedly."

"Thanks Gwen," I said. "I really appreciate this."

"No problem," she said with a smile. "It's nice to have someone who works here interested in the history of the Castle."

I stopped at the Roman Pool before going to the warehouse. I whispered, "Hello, I'm back" while standing at the spot where I'd first seen the glowing ball floating above the water. Nothing happened. I waited and called again, this time a little louder.

Maybe he followed me from the alcove where the water is shallow to here I thought. I walked into the alcove and called again. Within seconds, the glow coalesced over the water.

"Hello," I said.

"Hello. It's nice of you to come back."

"You asked me to come back so I did." I paused trying to decide on how to say it. "I think I know your name." The color drained from the orb, then slowly came back a pale pink. I waited until the color steadied, then slowly and distinctly said, "I think your name is Edward Brown."

The orb got brighter and the color morphed into purple. "Edward Alexander Brown," I heard the words slowly form around me. The orb began to dim.

I was afraid he was leaving me. I blurted out the rest. "My name is Catherine Mary Fallon ... of Bolton, Iowa." The orb brightened, time to go for broke. "My mother is Stephanie Anne Brown — your niece."

The orb cycled through all the colors of the rainbow and disappeared. I waited until my breathing went back to normal and the afterimage of the orb disappeared from my retina before leaving the pool.

I stopped at the Roman Pool three times over the next two weeks. I'd call and Uncle Edward, for that's how I thought of the orb now, would appear. Then I'd read him the names from the list to see if they were familiar. Some were, many weren't. It took a while. I'd have to read them slowly and carefully and provide him information that I'd been able to glean. Sometimes he seemed to know a name, but his response was confusing. "Clark Gable," I'd said. "He is an actor."

"Yes, I know him," Edward replied. "I met him in his underwear."

"In his underwear?"

"Oh yes," he said sounding very confident — which was unusual. "We were admiring the moon over the ocean."

Another one that got a reaction was Pamela Hudson. "Not her name," he said.

"That's the name on the list."

"Not her name," he repeated, then he faded away.

Chapter 13

Saturday found me back at the warehouse —
not for love of my job, but in search of a bookmark.
This bookmark was not the heavy paper strip
advertising the name, address, and phone number of
a bookstore commonly inserted into books at
purchase. This was a shiny enameled brass
Christmas gift my grandmother gave me when I
started college. I'd used it to mark my spot in Auntie
Mame, the novel I'd been reading on my lunch break.
I remembered when Dr. Lowe yelled out the back
door of the warehouse, "We can start working any
time now Miss Fallon." I slammed the book shut. I
decided that's when I must have lost it.

Curiously, Dr. Lowe's car was parked in its
usual spot next to the warehouse. I didn't care. I
wasn't going inside, only around the back. When I got
out of my car, a burly, crew-cut man jumped out of

Lowe's car. His hand clamped around my arm like a vice.

"Vere are you going?" he rasped.

"Stop! Keep away from me," I screamed. I slashed out with my free hand at his face. He caught my wrist. I tried to bite him. He twisted my arms down until I wept with the pain.

"Pieter! Stop!" Dr. Lowe bellowed from the warehouse door. The brute looked at Lowe, then pushed me away. I staggered back against the warehouse, slid away from the man along the warehouse wall, and into my car. I drove away, hot tears in my eyes.

I drove to Dave's Sweet Shoppe, the ice cream shop where April and I went after Mass for lunch and a sundae. I sat in the car for a while, maybe 15 minutes, before I felt I could get out without making a scene. I called Adam.

We met at Andre's that evening. Andre's, a restaurant decidedly down-scale from the Mountain Roost, was owned by the father of Adam's friend from law school. Adam had told me at our first dinner at the Mountain Roost that he was going to law school at night. The restaurant owner agreed to keep a table in an alcove reserved for Adam on the nights we needed to meet. The table sat a little away from other tables. It impressed me as a rendezvous for secret lovers. Still, we were able to converse without much chance of being overheard.

I thought I was under control, but I got a little weepy when I related the story. Poor Adam got a dirty look from the couple at a nearby table who must have thought it was his fault.

He laid out five photographs in front of me. "Are any of these men the man who was at the warehouse?" I looked them all over carefully, but my first impression was right.

"Him," I said pointing to the photo.

Adam took out his little notebook and wrote.

"Who is it?" I said.

"They are all people Lowe is known to associate with." I gave him an exasperated look. "His name is Pieter Vogelwaldt. He's Dutch. I can't say anything else. I'm sorry. I didn't expect you to ever be in physical danger by helping us."

My emotions — anger, fear, frustration — flashed through me in an instant. I sighed. "This didn't have anything to do with me helping you. I went there to find something I'd lost, the bookmark that my

Grandmother gave me."

We waved away the waiter who came to take our dessert order and we left in silence.

Chapter 14

I stood as Father Antonio gave the final blessing. The little church of Santa Rosa in Cambria was growing on me. It didn't have the grandeur of the Cathedral of the Holy Cross where I went to mass in Boston. Nor was it homey like Saint Mary's in Bolton, Iowa, steeped in two decades worth of personal history. Still, I was becoming familiar with it and it was becoming familiar with me.

The first time that I came, the stares of the parishioners were frank with curiosity. April recognized me and invited me to sit with her. Now the stares were replaced by smiles and nods of recognition, except those of a few young men who seemed to be working up their courage to introduce themselves. So far, none had found that courage.

Today April stood three pews in front of me with her fiancé Joe. Joe, who was nearing the end of a three-month long training assignment in San Diego, was home for a long weekend. I sat alone to give April and Joe their time together.

One pew in front and across the aisle stood Jack's sister Loraine and her fiancé Mark, her arm through his. I'd met her once when I was on a date with Jack. He had to go back to his house for gas money and she came out to say hello. She adroitly disentangled their arms to make the sign of the cross one last time, then they held hands.

The cantor announced the final hymn, Amazing Grace. All at once I felt lonely. At school there was always another grad student who would go to a museum or gallery or just talk about art. At home there were family and old high-school friends. Here the girls cared mostly about boys and, so far, the guys had been too shy to approach me. Except Jack, but he was such a klutz about it, I found it hard to take him seriously.

With a little start of recognition, I saw Adam slip from a pew near the door and join the crowd leaving the church. He waited for me outside.

"Mrs. Rogers said you would be here. Convenient. I hadn't gotten to Mass yet today," Adam said.

I felt curious eyes on us. I looped my arm through his and walked away from the parking lot towards the grotto where an elderly Spanish lady dressed in black was praying the rosary.

"What is it?" I asked when we were alone.

"I'm going to LA to look at a painting. The man who brought it to the gallery said the seller claims it is from the Hearst collection. I thought — if you are free — that you could come with me to authenticate it and verify the Hearst connection."

I had laundry to do, but Adam's offer sounded better than an afternoon washing lady's unmentionables. "I'm free. I'd like to go. Give me 15 minutes to walk home and change, then pick me up at the Rogers's house."

"I'll drive you home."

"No. You've already created a stir by showing up here. This town has a grapevine that makes Western Union weep with envy. Pick me up in 15 minutes."

When I came down the stairs 20 minutes later, Mrs. Rogers presented me with a paper sack and a thermos.

"Sandwiches and iced tea for the trip," she said. "Since you will be late, I made Mr. Spencer promise to buy you dinner."

"We're only going to look at a painting," I said sounding a little defensive.

"There's no way you will get back from Los Angles by dinner time so he should buy you dinner. Now get on. He is in the parlor with Albert."

They were looking at the pictures of the Rogers' children. I cleared my throat in my most ladylike manner. Adam shook Mr. Rogers's hand. "Good day sir," he said. We drove to San Luis Obispo to catch the train to LA.

The gallery owner, Ethan Wooster, met us at the door probably worried that his customers would see a cop and his fearless assistant and be spooked. Obviously relieved that we were not dressed as the boys in blue, he still hustled us into a back room quickly. There he introduced his researcher, a thin woman named Darlene Williams who didn't appear to spend much time in the California sun.

The object in question, an oil painting, sat on a large, blue-felt covered bench propped up against a table easel. A glint of recognition flashed in my head. A flashlight, magnifying glass, and loupe were on the bench. I picked up the flashlight and began my examination. Darlene hovered like a shadow. She'd likely expressed her opinion on the bona fides of the painting and was anxious to hear what I had to say.

I looked it over, especially around the edges, found the indistinct signature and date that may have been 1895. "That is Williams Clark Winton's *Maid Marian*. It's been cleaned and this isn't the original frame. It's genuine in my opinion."

"That was our opinion also," the Gallery owner said just a little testy. "Is it from the Hearst collection?"

"It's not something that would appeal to Hearst. He might have bought it for Marion Davies if it reminded him of a role she did."

The glint of recognition came back, stronger. I backed up a few feet to take in the whole painting. The light came on.

I strode back to the bench and put the painting face down on the felt. The back was a single sheet of wood sanded to a glass like finish. I ran a finger over the surface. A little down from the top left corner I felt it. "There," I said.

Adam ran his fingers over the back. "What? It's a little rough there. What is it?"

"That's the residue of a Savoy Gallery Auction sticker. If you have the auction catalogs here, look at the one for the summer 1956."

Mr. Wooster turned and said, "Darlene ...." The woman, who moved silently, was already gone. All eyes were on me for an eternity, only a half minute really, until she returned with the August 1956 Auction Catalog opened to the page with a picture of the painting.

"Hearst may have owned the painting and sold it in the late 1930's when he had to raise money," I said.

"Yes, well thank you Miss Fallon. My client said that the seller claimed the painting had been stolen recently. We will call Savoy tomorrow to verify the provenance and give him the news." Mr. Wooster sounded cautiously relieved. Darlene appeared visibly relieved.

"Savoy will be happy to give you the information," I said. "Provenance is a big part of any art gallery's reputation."

We ate tacos at the Union Station waiting for the train to San Luis Obispo, greasy sauce dripping through my fingers. They tasted great. "Maybe I can't get a decent bagel in California, but I'd never even heard of tacos in Boston. It's best we don't tell Mrs.

Rogers that this is the dinner you bought me."

"Why not?"

"She wouldn't consider you husband material giving me a dinner like this. She'd hang up on you when you call."

He arched his eyes. "Husband material?"

"I think she promised my mother to look out for my welfare. You know what that means — finding me a husband. They talk on the phone occasionally — mother to mother. Mrs. Rogers doesn't push. Just every now and again I do get a gentle nudge." I smiled at the idea. Adam grunted.

I finished the taco and licked my fingers clean one by one. "This behavior would not do at a Manhattan opening," I said. Adam laughed.

"Tell me, how did you know how to find that painting in the Savoy catalog? You impressed Wooster ... and you impressed me."

Now I laughed. "I had a good friend in grad school whose father was a partner at Savoy. She asked him to get us summer jobs at the gallery. She spent most of her summer flirting with a junior partner. I checked the catalog against the items to be auctioned. It would be a major embarrassment to have a catalog error show up at an auction. This painting was one I checked."

"I assume you did your job well by the way you recognized that painting."

"So did she. They were married last semester break and she's going to have a baby soon." I wiped my fingers with a napkin.

"So," I said, "why would someone claim they had a stolen Hearst painting for sale?"

"They think that the notoriety will add to the price. It might work and the upside is that if the police are called in, they can't be arrested for selling a painting that isn't stolen."

Adam opened his wallet and took out a train schedule. "They will call our train soon."

A picture of a pretty woman flashed by as he closed the wallet. "Who's she? Mrs. Spencer?" I asked. The tacos sat leaden in my stomach. Intellectually, I didn't care if he was married, but it seemed some non-intellectual part of me thought differently.

He opened the wallet to the picture. "This is Adrianne, my little sister. Doesn't she look like Madam Fourment?"

There was a resemblance. My digestive juices flowed once more.

Adam smiled at the picture. "I was right. When I told her she looked like the woman in the Rubens, she thought I was saying she was fat. I had to borrow a book from the library and show her the picture before she would talk to me again.

"Since you are interested, let me show you a picture of Mrs. Spencer ... and Mr. Spencer, my mother and father. The prospects for another Mrs. Spencer are dim until I finish law school and pass the bar."

The loudspeaker called our train.

"Did you have fun with your boyfriend on Sunday?" Jack's voice was controlled casual.

"Boy friend?" I didn't know where he was going with this so I played dumb.

"I hear you were in church together like the other love birds." The casual was gone, replaced with a good dose of sullenness.

I sighed. I was afraid that Adam's presence at church would cause tongues to wag. "He's not my boyfriend, he's my cousin. We weren't at church together, we were at the same church for the same Mass. I didn't know he was there until I left. There was no date. We went to Los Angeles to an art gallery to look at a painting he was interested in and absolutely none of this is your business!" I'd worked myself into an angry snit.

"Sorry," he said, but he didn't sound sorry.

Chapter 15

"Cathy, your mother is on the phone" Mrs. Rogers called singsong from the kitchen.

I hurried to the phone. Why had my mother called? In a week I'd be leaving to come home for Christmas. What was so important it couldn't wait? Long-distance calls were expensive and almost always meant bad news.

"Mom. What's the matter? What's wrong?"

"Nothing's wrong Cathy dear. I wanted to give you some news. Bud and Sally are getting married right after Christmas."

"Married? So soon?" Why hadn't I gotten an invitation by now or heard about an engagement?

"Yes. You'll want a new outfit. I hope you have time to shop out there. The wedding is the twenty-seventh." Mom sounded casual. Too casual. "I'm looking for something in blue myself."

"You haven't bought your dress yet? How long have you known about the wedding?"

"Oh, my. Look how long we've talked. It's too expensive to chit-chat long distance. I'll tell you all about it when you get home. Bye." She was gone. Only the static on the long distance connection remained.

"Is everything all right back home?" asked Mrs. Rogers when I came back into the living room. Mr. Rogers dipped the corner of his newspaper a fraction.

"My brother's getting married on the twenty-seventh. I'll have to find a new dress to wear to the wedding."

Mrs. Rogers's eyes shot to her husband for an instant. The corner of his paper moved up to its original position. She smiled. "Well isn't that wonderful. I know a lovely dress shop in San Luis Obispo. Let me write down the directions."

It was after dinner on the day I'd come home before I could talk to Mom alone. We were in the kitchen doing the dishes. I'd insisted on helping her and, of course, Dad graciously left us by ourselves. Bud ran off to Sally's house.

Mom washed and I dried. As usual. No matter

how many years I'd spent in college and even now that I had a job and was living half a continent away, at home I was still the baby of the family. I helped Mrs. Rogers with the dishes when I was home for dinner. Usually she washed, although sometime when her legs hurt, I'd wash and she would sit on a stool and dry. One week, Mrs. Rogers went to visit her sister in Sacramento. Mr. Rogers drove her there on Saturday and drove himself back on Sunday. That week I cooked us dinner and he dried the dishes as I washed. He had a lot to say while we worked and his wife wasn't around to dominate the conversation. He told me how he met his wife and about their children, but all history seemed to stop by December 6, 1941.

"Isn't this wedding a little rushed?" I asked.

"Depends on what you consider rushed," Mom said. The dishes were piled on the sink board — glassware and silverware first, then crockery, and pots last. That's the order dishes were always done so that the dishwater didn't get greasy too quickly. "It's fast if you need to observe all the niceties and proprieties. It's about the right speed if you want a decent interval between the wedding and the baby's arrival."

I nodded. I hadn't thought it through as fast as

Mrs. Rogers, but this was answer that made the most sense. I felt a curious pride in having figured it out.

"Are you and Dad mad at Bud?"

"No, not me. As your Grandma says, most babies take nine months to be born. First babies come whenever they want. Your father isn't happy, but he doesn't seem to remember himself at Bud's age."

In spite of myself, I did the arithmetic. Bud had been born more than a year after they were married.

"Your dad was just lucky not to get the most fertile filly in the corral. Only the prettiest." She smiled to herself.

We did dishes in silence for a while.

Mom let the water out of the sink and refilled it with fresh dishwater for the pots. "I hope you're not upset that you're not in the wedding party. It would have been hard to get a bridesmaid dress made up for you in time."

"No. I understand. Besides, Sally and I weren't good friends in high school." Sally and I had graduated the same year, but we ran in different circles. My circle had more books than boys. "And from the first pew, I'll be able to see if Bud can actually say 'I do' without his knees shaking."

The pots took more of Mom's concentration. We worked in silence until they were finished. Afterward we sat down at the kitchen table for a second cup of coffee. Mom got up and tiptoed to the door looking down the hall toward the Living Room where Dad was watching TV. She came back, opened a cabinet door, and took out a bottle of Irish whiskey. She poured a generous shot in each coffee cup.

"We have another bottle for Christmas dinner. Your father always likes to make a big show of opening a new bottle. I don't know what he thinks I do with the half empty ones. I have to get rid of them somehow."

I'd forgotten the burn of the whiskey. I guess I've been drinking too much wine since I moved to California.

"Wow. An extra Irish coffee this year. I'm on the road to perdition," I said. It felt good. Warm. The warm weather of California had made me soft ... the cold of the early Midwest winter had cut into me deeply. Fortunately, my old sweaters were still in my room.

"So what about you? Is there somebody in your life? Don't tell me nobody and nothing because Mrs. Rogers told me that you go out with somebody.

Maybe two somebodies."

"I'll have to talk to Mrs. Rogers. She said she doesn't gossip about her boarders."

"That's what she said to me as well, but she also said she won't refuse to answer a direct question from a mother."

I laughed. "She does take care of me."

"That isn't an answer to my question."

"Oh, there is this guy. He works up at the castle. He's cute and nice, but hard to take seriously. He'd rather be surfing."

Mom shook her head. "I read about them surfers in the Sunday Supplement. They sound like a strange bunch."

"Jack's not too strange. His father owns the bank in town. How strange can he be?" I hoped Mom didn't pursue this too far or I might have to tell her about him being arrested for vagrancy. "And we're not serious. At least I'm not." That last bit sounded lame.

"And the other somebody?" Mom asked?

The cousin story wasn't going to work on her. "He's a lawyer who is interested in art. We get together and discuss paintings every now and again. He's a bit older." Wow, that was a stretch, but Mom accepted it.

Mom got up and washed out her coffee cup in the sink. "California doesn't sound like much of a state if the best a smart, beautiful girl like you can find is a surfer bum and an old guy who only wants to talk about paintings."

"Well Mom," I said bringing my coffee cup to the sink, "a working woman doesn't have much time to socialize."

Was that really my brother standing at the altar? He looked mature. He'd always looked older to me, but this was the first time he looked mature. When had that happened?

Sally glowed. Her sisters — bridesmaids and maid of honor — reflected her sunshine. Last night, at the rehearsal dinner, she hugged me and said, "I'm so happy that you could be here." Then she added *sotto voce*, "Aunt Cathy."

Grandma sat on my right. She looked good. Alert. Not as frail as when I'd seen her last. I guess she was like the retired fire horse that perked up every time she heard the alarm. The prospect of a new mother and baby in the family stirred her juices.

I looked to the left at Mom and Dad. Mom looked happy. Dad? Dad's appearance was more complex. He smiled a subdued smile. He watched the ceremony, but behind his eyes, I could see him mapping out the future. Sally's people were farmers. Four girls, no boys. The burden of farming would go to the husband of one of them. Bud? Who knows. If Bud, who would take over our family business?

The mantle of family lay more heavily on my shoulders than it had just a couple of weeks ago. So this was growing up? Somehow it didn't feel as much fun as it had when I first left home to go to college.

"For better or for worse," Bud said.

"For richer or for poorer," prompted the priest.

"For richer or for poorer."

"In sickness and in health."

"Til death do us part." Bud spoke loud, clear, sincere.

I looked at his knees. Rock solid. I looked at Mom and Dad. They held hands. Mom cried.

I thought of myself up at the altar hearing Jack say those words. Could I see that? Then Bud and Sally kissed and the organ blasted out the wedding march.

Aunt Peg leaned over from the pew behind me. "So Cathy, when do we get to see you married?" The questions were starting.

Chapter 16

Tuesday morning dawned gloriously — for Iowa, but just another average day in San Simeon. The warehouse was quiet. After noon, Dr. Lowe had gone. He'd received a phone call, "summoned, like a servant," he described it, to a meeting at the Administration building. "Please ... don't get into any trouble," he said as if instructing a ten year old.

The Jacks had retrieved all the designated paintings from the back of the warehouse, so I quickly examined what remained and returned them to their crates. There weren't very many and without Dr. Lowe's meticulous, plodding inspections which never found anything, there was no reason for the task to take long. I decided to prowl the warehouse, checking out the rest of the paintings we still had to assess before I called the Castle for Big Jack and Jack to put away the day's work.

The rows of unexamined paintings stretched a disheartening length, at least if you believed that we had to get through all of them before the Castle opened to the public. We didn't, at least that was the rumor. Jack heard through the Castle grapevine that the state officials had decided to go with what was already hung for the initial exhibit and re-evaluate if Dr. Lowe ever finished. And they were going to hold Dr. Lowe to his contract to evaluate all the paintings no matter how long it took and there would be no additional payment. I hoped the no additional payment part didn't apply to me. I wondered if Dr. Lowe was getting the word now.

I wandered through the crates reading the labels. Most were nailed shut, but some had latches and hinges so that they could be opened easily without damaging either the painting or the crate. Some I opened because I recognized the artist, others because the name of the painting sounded intriguing. One small crate was labeled *An Afternoon Stroll*, George Sheridan Knowles, Watercolor. I opened it up and carried it to a window so I could better see it in the light.

It was exquisite. In the foreground, two well quaffed young ladies, elegantly dressed in late 18th

Century gowns strolled on a formal veranda. In the background, two formally dressed men were engaged in conversation with another woman. It took my breath away.

I heard the town clock strike three. Time to call the Jacks. I put the watercolor back in its case and latched it shut.

Dr. Lowe was spending more time at the Administration building, which made his mood very black. Today he was summoned in the morning just after he pulled the set of invoices for the paintings to be evaluated. He stormed out to his car. His histrionics were old hat by now, so much so, his usual parting comment, "Please don't get into trouble" was barely offensive.

I looked through the small pile of invoices for the paintings we needed to examine today, then noticed the clipboard with the rest of the invoices still lay on the desk. This represented a major breach of protocol ... the clipboard was always kept in a desk drawer, forbidden territory for a mere mortal like me. And the top invoice on the clipboard was the watercolor I'd seen a couple of weeks ago and loved so. I took it off the clipboard and put the clipboard into the desk drawer.

I went back into the warehouse and began matching paintings to the invoices. When I came to the watercolor, I went to the area where I'd seen it last. Missing. I looked around the immediate area. Still missing. Finally I walked the rows and rows of crated paintings. Definitely missing. I called the Castle for the two Jacks and wondered what was going on.

When Dr. Lowe came back I told him I couldn't find one of the paintings. When I showed him the invoice, he went into a spastic rage. He would never have given me this particular invoice, he said. Where did I get it? I played dumb. That's what he deserved for treating me the way he did. No I didn't touch the clipboard. It was in the desk drawer as usual. Maybe you included the invoice accidentally. You were upset this morning. He muttered and fumed. Since I'd almost finished the examinations, he gave me the rest of the day off.

I wondered. Could this be one of the unusual events Adam was interested in? I stopped in Cambria before going to the Roger's house. I went into the Savings and Loan and changed a couple of dollar bills for nickels, dimes, and quarters, then I went into the Dave's Sweet Shoppe and called Adam's number.

Not in, so I left a message. When I got home there was a message from Adam — meet him for dinner at Andre's.

We sat at our table in the alcove. Over dinner, I told Adam the story. Mostly he listened and wrote things down in his notebook. He went back over the story verifying the details. When had I seen the painting ... about two weeks ago. When did I notice it missing ... today. Why did I take the invoice from the clipboard ... because I wanted to see the painting again. Describe the painting exactly ... two ladies foreground, two men and another lady background, elegant 17th Century clothes. Who painted the picture ... George Sheridan Knowles. Finally he put the notebook away.

"It may be nothing. It does seem like an over reaction. Still, from what you say he is a strange guy so maybe this is normal for him. Could he be worried somebody stole the painting and he will be held accountable."

"I don't think he is worried about being held accountable," I said. Dessert had been served and I was eating a piece of apple pie with my coffee. Àla mode! I made a mental note to only have dry toast for breakfast for the next couple of days to make up for this. "We have come across three or four invoices that we couldn't match to paintings since I've been here and know that there were others before I came. We report them as missing. Apparently there was a lot of missing pieces with the statues and other artwork as well. The accounting wasn't great around this artwork, especially when Hearst had to sell some of his collection in 1937 to raise money."

"Well, keep your eyes open and let me know if anything else happens. And thank you."

I swallowed the last piece of apple pie and primly wiped my lips. Adam was right ... Andre's looked a bit like a dump, but the cook was a prince.

The next Monday, 9 A.M. sharp, I arrived at the warehouse and found Dr. Lowe already there. "See," he said pointing triumphantly at a crate on the table. "The painting was here all the time. I arrived early this morning and decided to look for it."

Dr. Lowe at work early was enough of an unusual event to make it reportable to Adam. And the watercolor suddenly found? Too much of a coincidence for me. I called Adam after work from Dave's Sweet Shoppe.

"He never comes in early?" he said.

"Not in the eight months that I've been there."

"Hmmm. Well it may or may not mean anything. Let me know ... and thanks."

Three days later, Dr. Lowe got another summons to go to the Castle. Without him, I quickly completed the painting assessments for the day, went into the back of the warehouse, and located the watercolor. I wanted to be sure it was there and to admire the beauty of the scene. I found and opened the crate, took the painting out, and examined it carefully. It was every bit as beautiful as I remembered. I examined the frame inch by inch, first the front and then the back. Finally I examined the edge. Along the bottom was a bit of something which I dug out with my fingernail. The pungent smell of oil paint hit my nostrils. Most of the spot was under my nail, but a little remained on the frame caught in a crevice. I rubbed. Burnt umber spread across my finger. Very strange.

I cleaned the frame with my hankie, then cleaned my fingers. I put the painting away and went back to the office. I was just calling Big Jack and Jack when Dr. Lowe stormed in.

"Take the rest of the day off," he barked. I didn't need to be told twice.

I met Adam at Andree's. "What's so important you had to see me?" Adam asked. He didn't sound annoyed, just businesslike.

"I went to look at the watercolor again today and I got some dirt under my fingernails."

Now he looked annoyed, but didn't say anything. I took my hankie out and laid it on the table. I dug the bit of paint from under my fingernail with my nail file and then spread it out.

"That's oil paint," he said. He sniffed it, then picked up the hankie and held it close to his face examining it. "I need this."

"What a girl doesn't sacrifice for a free meal," I said and smiled. "I figured you would. I brought another."

Then he began to ask questions walking me through locating and examining the watercolor. "So you think the paint could have been on there when you examined it with Dr. Lowe last week?"

"Yes. We look at the painting mostly to see if there is a need for cleaning or conservation. We give the front of the frame, the part that the public would see if it were hanging in the Castle, a quick look to see if any repairs are needed. This bit of oil paint was on the side in a crevice. It could have easily been overlooked."

"I'll have the lab be sure it is oil paint, although it sure looks and smells that way. Maybe they can tell me how old it is." He looked at me. "Thanks."

Chapter 17

Jack worked alone moving bags of fertilizer and mulch from the parking lot where he and Big Jack had unloaded them from the truck. Big Jack had driven back to town to get more leaving Jack to load them onto a cart and bring them to the beds where the gardeners would be working tomorrow.

Donkey work. Still, Jack wasn't unhappy. The breeze coming out of the west cooled him and carried the sweet smell of the ocean. Sweat glistened on his forehead and collected in the valley of his spine as he worked under the clear sky. Visions of barrel waves, inspired by the perfume of the sea on the breeze, dominated his thoughts. Someday ... Hawaii, Australia. He'd ride those waves, feel the bucking board under his feet, watch the wave curl above and around him as he crouched on the board and outraced the collapsing tunnel of water behind him.

He mopped his forehead with a red and white polka dotted handkerchief. A splat of color caught his eye — Cathy's funny little car parked near the Roman Pool. Cathy. When he was with her, he forgot about surfing. More often now, he thought about her when she wasn't around. Sometimes she was the cause of a sleepless night. She wasn't like the other girls who hung out with the surfers. They were giggly and flighty; hanging on one guy, flitting to another, going off together like they were beach grass blowing in the sea breeze. Cathy was Cathy. She did what she did, sometimes motivated by thoughts that Jack couldn't fathom.

Like hanging around the Roman Pool. The realization came over him like a wave made of clouds. He must have seen her car parked up here a dozen times. After the campout, Jack would have guessed that she wouldn't want to go near the pool ever again. The couple of times Jack had seen her and not just the car, she was wearing her work clothes. She carried no bundle with a towel and swimsuit and her hair wasn't wet when she left.

Curious, Jack dropped the bag of fertilizer on the pile and headed towards the Roman Pool.

Inside, he silently closed the door and listened.

Whispers. The bare tile walls made locating the source problematical. He could see the main part of the pool from the door and Cathy was nowhere to be seen. He hesitated. He knew he had the knack of doing the wrong thing when he was with Cathy. A pang in the back of his brain told him he didn't want to do something else to arouse her disapproval. But now Jack was curious and he was almost never curious.

One of the sounds sounded like a sob. *You've got to help* shouted the comic book superhero from his childhood drowning out the whisper of reason from the wiser angels of his spirit.

He padded around the pool, silent as a thief in the night.

The whispers grew louder as he approached the alcove. Who was she whispering to? Jack could only hear her. Jack, edging to the corner, looked in the alcove. Cathy sat cross-legged near the edge, her body facing the water. Her face was turned towards his and she looked directly into his eyes as if she knew he was going to be there. Face flushed. Jaw set. Not embarrassed. Angry.

"What are you doing? Spying on me?" She spoke in a forceful whisper. Jack would have preferred a shout. Then he would know she was letting her anger out. Jack felt like he was staring at a boiler watching the over-pressure valve trying to open.

"Uh." Jack made a noise, but couldn't come up with anything to say.

Cathy slid herself away from the pool's edge until her back touched the wall, folded her arms across her chest, and leaned a little forward to glare at him.

Jack couldn't comprehend. This was the most little girl action he had ever seen from her. What was she doing that embarrassed her so?

Jack stood rigid where he was. He'd experienced her moods before — happy, sad, angry, curious, distant, skeptical. The memory of her angry embarrassment when her swimsuit turned all but transparent still caused him to cringe. He'd never seen this — embarrassed, ashamed with no defense. Relief flooded his body, relief that he would not be assaulted for interrupting her. Next came the need to comfort her tempered by caution, the fear that being too solicitous would trigger a reaction.

"I'm sorry Cathy," he said voice not much above a whisper. "My boss had me hauling bags of fertilizer all morning. I saw your car and just came in

154

to say hello and cool down. I thought I heard you talking to someone, maybe crying. I wanted to be sure you were OK." He talked low and earnest like he talked to his baby cousin when the little girl cried.

Cathy stared back at Jack. He saw no anger in her eyes. What was there? Indecision? Anxiety?

Silence filled the space between them.

"Who were you talking to?" Jack asked.

Cathy broke eye contact, but not before Jack saw the embarrassment come back.

"Were you praying?" Jack knew that Cathy was religious. April, who was religious and a prude said she met Cathy at Santa Rosa Catholic Church on Sunday and after Mass they would go to Dave's Sweet Shoppe for lunch and a cream soda.

Cathy made a noise that could have been a snort of derision or a quick laugh.

Confusion raged within Jack. His sister had advised him to listen, be empathetic. It was more work than he expected, especially since Cathy wouldn't talk.

He sat cross-legged at the edge of the pool, back to the water. "I just want to help if I can."

She turned back to him, her eyes wary.

"Do you? You'll laugh at me."

"No," he said adjusting his voice to match her near whisper. "I can't imagine laughing at you."

Cathy sighed, relaxed the arms crossed over her chest until her hands were folded in her lap, and looked up at the ornate ceiling.

"I had an uncle — a great-uncle really, my grandmother's brother. Great-Uncle Edward. He came to San Simeon once in 1936. He worked for Hearst and came to see him for some reason, on business I suppose.

Jack relaxed. Cathy wasn't quite herself, but she didn't sound like a bomb ready to explode.

"Makes sense," Jack said. "Hearst often had employees here during the week ..."

"He was murdered. Right here! Stabbed in the chest as he rounded the corner." Cathy pointed with limp motion to the corner Jack had rounded when he came in.

In the silence, small waves splashed against the side of the pool.

"Wow," Jack said. "I never heard of anyone being murdered at the Castle. Hearst must have gone nuts. He wouldn't even let them use traps that would kill the mice."

"The police found his body in Glendale near

the train station. They said it was a robbery gone bad."

"Then why do you think he died here?" Jack heard the skepticism in his voice and tried to change the tone to reason. "If the police ..."

"Because ...," Cathy said and took a deep breathe, "because he told me. You remember the night of the campout? I went around the corner to dive. After I dove, I was sitting on the side of the pool and he came to me."

"A ghost?" Jack said.

"No, not a chain rattling, moaning ghost. It wasn't like Christmas Carol. He was more like a spirit. A ball. It hovered over the water and glowed a little. The water around it rippled."

There was silence as Jack absorbed this. He had always idolized Cathy as smart and sophisticated. Now he was trying to fit loony tunes into the picture.

"Are you all right Cathy?" Jack asked. His tone was sincere as was his feeling. "You do spend a lot of time in that closed up warehouse with Dr. Lowe. I hear he smokes those funny little cigarettes in that fancy holder. Just smelling that smoke can make you feel odd."

Cathy was staring at him again. There seemed to be a glow in her eyes. All at once, Jack was frightened.

"Maybe we should go before we are missed," he said rising awkwardly from his cross-legged position. Behind him an orb of bright light glowed deep red. Ripples, wavelets of water flowed to a position under the orb, swelling directly below it. The water formed itself into a watermelon-sized ball that flew to the spot where Jack's head had been a moment before, hitting him in the back. Reflexively, Jack pushed back against the water and toppled backwards in the pool.

Jack heard Cathy's laughter echo through the cavern of the pool when he splashed to the surface. Relief. Cathy sounded normal.

He pulled himself out of the pool. "Did you do that?" he asked.

She laughed again. "No silly. How could I." Then in a horse whisper, "Don't make Uncle Edward angry again."

"Let's get out of here," Jack said and taking her hand, leading the way to the door. Outside in the warm, bright day they made their way towards Cathy's car still holding hands.

Big Jack's truck pulled up and he jumped out and eyed them. "What have you two been up to?"

"I was in the Roman Pool having lunch. Jack came in to get out of the sun and cool down after the slave labor you left him to do. I helped him out by pushing him in the pool," Cathy said with a mischievous smile. She released Jack's hand, said goodbye to the two men, and went to her car.

Jack watched her go and wondered. Wondered over the ease of the lie. Wondered where the blast of water had come from. Wondered about the story of the ghost of her Uncle Edward. Wondered if he knew Cathy at all.

Chapter 18

Lowe sent me from the warehouse on a fool's errand to inventory the art on the second floor of the Casa de Sol. There was a copy of the inventory for the whole house in the files, but no, he wanted an eyeball check to be sure. No wonder we fell further and further behind schedule.

I screeched the tires on my little Nash as I left the parking lot. *Calm down*, I thought. *Don't let him get to you. When life gives you lemons, make lemonade.* I had to laugh. Only twenty-four years old, I sounded like my mother. Well, it was lunchtime so why not stop at the Administration Building to have lunch with the girls.

I found them outside at the picnic table, five of them, clustered around April. April was getting married in six weeks — my invitation arrived yesterday.

"Maybe they taught a course in *that* at Radcliffe," Clarissa said, "or she learned it from a Harvard guy." Clarissa smiled saccharine sweet at me.

"I learned Harvard guys think they're prettier than their date." They all giggled. "Sometimes they are. What's this all about?"

Mary Claire leaned across the table to get closer to me, a conspiratorial smirk on her face. "April is worried about what to do on her wedding night. You know, after the lights go out." There were a couple of nervous giggles, including mine.

"G' day ladies." Phoebe said in her delightful accent. She squeezed in at the end of the table. We all turned towards her.

"April is worried about her wedding night," Mary Claire repeated. "You're married Phoebe. What was your wedding night like?"

Phoebe stopped unwrapping her sandwich and looked at us. As usual, she smiled. She was perennially cheerful. "Which 'ne? I was married three times, wasn't I?"

There were gasps and an "Oh".

"The first time I was 18, to a boy who I knew since I was seven. We got married in '39. He'd joined the army and was going to be shipped to France to fight the Boche." Blank faces stared at Phoebe. "Boche! The Germans! England and France declared war on Germany in 1939 after the Germans invaded Poland. We had three weeks together, then he went to France."

Her smile faded. "He spent the winter in a trench waiting for the fighting to start. Sitzkrieg they called it. The Phony War. It got real soon enough. The Germans attacked in the spring and pushed the English army to the channel. He was wounded and evacuated off the beach at Dunkirk, but he bled to death before he reached England." Everyone fell silent. "So my girl friends took me out for a piss-up, that's a drunk to you Yanks, and I woke up in the morning next to an RAF pilot. He flew bombers, not Spitfires, so he wasn't involved in all the Battle of Britain stuff. I moved to the town next to his air base."

"Did you get married?" April said.

We got married, were together for four years. Then, just after Christmas 1944 his bomber took a direct hit from antiaircraft fire. The bombs exploded. Nobody survived."

Phoebe took an apple from her lunch bag and studied it. She found a spot that didn't seem to meet with her approval and polished it to a high gloss. "So on New Years Eve I went out and got really pissed again. I woke up in my bed-sitter with an American Major sleeping in the armchair. He'd taken me home and watched over me because he wanted to be sure I was OK. That's what he said and it must have been true since I still had me knickers on." She stopped and eyed the blank stares. "Knickers. Underpants. Now do you understand?"

A bit red faced, we nodded.

"So he spent the rest of the war being sure I was OK and I spent the rest of the war with me knickers still on. At first I thought he was married, but I found out he wasn't. After Germany surrendered, he stayed on to help shut down the air base and move all the equipment back to America."

"What happened to him?" April was wide-eyed and breathless.

Phoebe's smile returned. "I lured him to my room with the offer of a cup of tea. I kissed him and told him I loved him and he'd better ravish me there and then or I was going to jump out the window. Thankfully, he made the right choice. That's how I got to California."

I realized that we'd all been leaning towards

Phoebe, open mouthed, to catch every word. We all sat upright and collectively caught our breath.

Still, Mary Claire hadn't gotten the answer to her original question and she was like a junkyard dog in pursuit of knowledge, as long as it was salacious. "You still didn't tell us what the wedding night was like."

"Ah well, during Queen Victoria's time, there was an instruction manual for women that covered it pretty well. If I remember correctly, the instructions were '... stare at the ceiling and think of England'."

We emitted a chorus of groans. A couple of girls I knew of at Radcliffe had "done it". Their vague reports had been glowing, but no more illuminating than Phoebe's description. Could they be believed? Would they report that the forbidden fruit was sour grapes? Still, Phoebe had married three times so there must be something there.

And there was Betty Tuttle. She went home to Philadelphia for the summer between her junior and senior years and came back married. She never told how or why. The rumor was that she had gotten pregnant. She and her boyfriend got married quickly, then she lost the baby or maybe it was a hysterical pregnancy, which was the other rumor. Either way, one late night in the dorm, me, Betty, and Sue-Anne Sutton were taking a vanilla ice cream and chocolate syrup break from studying. Betty scrapped the last of her ice cream and chocolate syrup from her bowl, licked her spoon, and said, "Um that's good, but not as good as sex." Sue-Anne gagged on her ice cream and we beat her back until she began to breathe again. We never got any more information out of Betty, but the phrase became our private joke.

Phoebe went back to her sandwich. "Don't look so down, girls. Find the right chap and it will be a voyage of discovery. Don't be embarrassed to tell him what he does that you like and listen to what he says he likes. Things may take a while, but it will be wonderful ... with the right chap." Phoebe took a bite of tuna salad on rye.

I could see Mary Claire trying to think of another way to ask the question. April spoke first. "I'm afraid of having a baby." Her voice was tiny. "I'm afraid of having a baby before me and Joe can make enough money for a house. I'm afraid we will be living in my parent's basement for years like my mother and father did, being miserable because we have no privacy and everyone's butting into our business."

A bird chirped in the silence. The breeze

flapped the leaves on a branch of the nearby Aspen tree. Phoebe swallowed. "Well, April, that is a concern. A good doctor will be able to help. I'll bring in the name of my doctor tomorrow."

A week later April stopped by the warehouse. "Hi. I saw your car outside so I knew you were here." Dr. Lowe rolled his eyes and stalked off to the office. April's voice dropped as she handed me a business card. "Here. This is Phoebe's doctor. He is good. Kind. His nurse is his wife and they have four married daughters. Joe and I don't need to worry about having a baby until we are good and ready. I got this card for you ... you know, you and Jack." April blushed as she said it.

"Jack?" I said. "Why?"

"Jack's sweet on you. I thought that you were sweet on him too. He said you were coming to the wedding with him."

Jack had asked me if I wanted him to drive us to the wedding. He was going to borrow his father's Cadillac. That sounded like a distinct improvement over either car we could muster, but hardly constituted a relationship.

"If Jack is sweet on me, he has a funny way of

showing it," I said. "He always acts so weird,"

"I've know Jack since fifth grade," April said softly and confidentially. "He's never acted like this around any other girl. He'd rather be surfing usually. You're special to him."

I looked at the card. Dr. Thomas Fieldstein. My mother did tell me to find a good doctor out here just in case. "Thanks for the card and thanks for the reading on Jack."

April look pleased.

"Don't expect much," I said. She smiled a radiant smile and left.

Chapter 19

Jack brought the note to me when he and Big Jack came to fetch the crates for the day's assessment.

"April asked me to give this to you." He handed me a cream-colored envelope about the size and shape of a wedding invitation. The paper was heavy. My name, care of 'Hearst Castle, San Simeon', was on the outside in an ornate hand. Except for the canceled three-cent stamp in the upper-right, the envelope most resembled a hand delivered invitation to the Ball from the Prince.

I put it in my purse and thanked him. I could see that curiosity was eating him alive. Well, a little mystery about a girl's life never hurt her image. Dr. Lowe hrumped impatiently. I was going to have to wait and so was Jack.

My lunch lay untouched on the picnic table outside the warehouse. I'd planned to wait until after work when I got back to the Rogers' house so I could open the envelope in the privacy of my room, but the cream envelope with the calligraphy address called to me in polite, formal, but insistent tones from my purse like a disapproving English Butler. I laid my lunch out as usual in an effort to contain a school-girl like curiosity. Finally, I took out the envelope, tore open the flap, and read.

March 18, 1958

Miss Fallon,

I would be pleased
to receive you at my house
on Saturday, March 22 at
11 am.

Marion

The letter was written in the same exquisite handwriting as the address on the envelope. The signature, by contrast, appeared childish — vertical and cramped.

With a more careful second look, I saw embossed at the top of the paper:

Marion Davies
1011 North Beverly Drive
Beverly Hills, California

I called Gwen from the phone booth across the street. Yes, she had a letter written and signed by Marion Davies. Yes, she would be in the office until five.

As usual, Dr. Lowe and I finished the day's quota at 3:30. I called the Jacks. They took their time and it was near 4:30 before they got into their truck and headed back to the Castle. I ran to my little car and before long, I'd caught up to them on the highway. On a straight section of Route 1, my poor car screaming in protest, I passed the truck.

I went straight to Gwen's office, barely acknowledging the greetings from the girls who were straightening their desks and getting ready to leave.

"Hi," said Gwen with her customary cheerfulness. "You look a bit out of breath."

"I didn't want to miss you. Not after you went to all the trouble of finding the letter for me."

"Oh no trouble." She picked a file folder from a pile on her desk and handed it to me.

The file contained a simple one-page note. The letterhead was a line drawing of the Casa del Mar, the guesthouse that faced the ocean. Above the picture was printed "LA CUESTA ENCHANDA" — the Enchanted Hill — Hearst's name for the complex. Below the picture, "CASA DEL MAR" and a little further below "SAN SIMEON, CAL".

The handwriting did not match the calligraphy in the note I received, but the simple signature "Marion" did.

With a spasm, I drew in a breath. I knew Marion Davies was still alive. I also knew, at some level, that Hollywood had a finely tuned grapevine. I had tracked down some of the names on the list and asked about that weekend. It had not occurred to me that my questions would shake that grapevine and the vibrations would reach the one person left who was most intimately concerned with Hearst and San Simeon.

"Are you OK?" Gwen asked, looking concerned. Neither college nor the gallery scene had prepared me for this level of surprise and I guess it showed.

"Oh, sure," I said smiling. The smile wasn't forced. Naive possibly, but not forced. I may have been slow to realize that Marion Davies still had friends who would alert her to my probing, but I deduced in an instant that she would probably get more information from me than I would get from her.

"Thanks so much Gwen. We'd both better go home for dinner."

After I gave the cabbie outside Union Station the address, he turned to give me an appraising look. "Are you a friend of Miss Davies?" he asked.

"No," I said. "We have an acquaintance in common. She asked me to see her so we could discuss him." *I'm becoming a good liar. What did that say about me.*

"She's a swell lady," he said putting the cab into gear and pulling smoothly into traffic without making me fear for my life like a Boston or New York cabbie. "I drove her to her place once when she came in by train. Class lady. Good tipper."

I'm sure the last comment was a hint for a good tip. Alas, the fare itself was $7.85 and I had only $25 to my name so I had to ask for 50 cents back from the $9 I handed him.

Once he drove off I confronted the enormous pink stucco structure at the far end of the drive. Well, I'd already invested much of my net worth for the rest of the month in this trip and had a peanut butter and jelly sandwich in my purse for lunch so what did I have to lose now? I walked up and rang the bell.

An immaculately dressed, gray-haired woman opened the door. "Miss Fallon," she said before I could say a word, "We are so pleased you could visit." She led me through the house and out to an open veranda that overlooked a two-tiered spillway that emptied into a pool. It was similar to the arrangement of the Neptune Pool at San Simeon.

She appeared a minute later with Marion Davies. Marion looked at me. Without turning she said, "Edith, bring us some tea."

Marion Davies appeared older than any of the pictures that I'd seen, but the pictures were mostly publicity stills from her movies in the 1930s and 1940s. Her hair and makeup were perfect, however, which immediately got me wondering about how my hair and makeup held up on the trip from Cambria. She was wearing a white silk pants outfit, probably pajamas. Why not. This was her back yard and the morning was warm. In fact, I was beginning to sweat under the scrutiny of her piercing eyes.

"So you're the little v-vi-vixen that's trying to dig up dirt on Poppy and me. Talking about murder at the Castle. That's bullshit. P-Poppy wouldn't allow it."

"Miss Davies, can I explain? I ..."

Edith came out and put a tray down on the table without it making a sound. She took a filled teacup from the tray and put it in front of Marion. Then she took an empty cup and filled it with tea from a steaming teapot. After leaving a plate of cookies and sweetbreads, she took the tray and withdrew.

Marion took a swallow from her cup. I smelled whiskey.

I took a deep breath. "My uncle was a Hearst employee. On August 28, 1936 he went to San Simeon. He stayed overnight Friday night and apparently left late Saturday or early Sunday without sleeping in his bed. He was found Sunday evening near the train station in Glendale. He'd been stabbed to death. I'm just trying to find out what I can."

She drank more from her cup. "You don't want to know about Ince? I've said everything I'm going to say about Ince." Thomas Ince was a producer who had died mysteriously on Hearst's yacht in 1927.

"No. It's about my uncle. Edward Brown. That's

all I care about."

She continued to stare at me. I felt awkward in the silence. I took a sip of my tea. It was hot. I burned my tongue.

"S-S-Sunday you say. That's not right. Employees came to the Castle during the week."

"I have a guest list from that weekend." I took it from my purse and showed it to her. I pointed to Edward Brown's name, producer crossed out and employee written in, the arrows indicating the change of room.

"I thought they threw these things out after the weekend was over."

"The police asked them to save it until the investigation was finished."

She eyed the list like it were a dead fish until ... softly, she said "Pamela Hudson. She's my niece. She wanted to be in movies so we invited her to the Ranch to meet some movie people and get a start."

She closed her eyes for a moment and I felt like she wasn't there. "I remember she was palling around with a guy who was a little older than she was. Do you have a picture of your uncle?"

"No, sorry." I shook my head. "Until I came out here, I didn't know I had an uncle who died in

California. He'd broken with the family." I let that trail off. No need to go into the "Chicago Woman."

"Maybe Pam can give you more information. Do you know how to find her?" I shook my head. Marion stood up. "Edith," she called. Before I could stand, Edith was there giving Marion an inquiring look.

"Find Pamela's address and give it to her," Marion indicated me with a tilt of her head, "and make sure she gets back to town." Marion Davies walked away without another look or word, teacup in hand.

"Please sit and I'll find the address. Have some more tea." Edith was the surrogate gracious hostess. "Do you have a car?"

"No," I said in a small voice, feeling deflated. "I took a taxi from Union Station."

"I'll have one of the men drive you." Edith disappeared into the bowels of the house.

Alone, I ate some of the sweetbreads with more gusto than was appropriate for polite company. I had to skip breakfast and drive my little car faster than it cared to go to catch the early train. A quick glance at my watch told me that I'd have no trouble being back for dinner.

Edith returned with a slip of paper for me. "Charles will drive you to the station." Charles wore a sports jacket with no tie and had dirt under his finger nails, a man-of-all-work I assumed.

We walked to the door. I asked "Edith, did you write the note to me ... and the envelope?"

"Yes."

"Your handwriting is beautiful."

"Thank you. It's a lost art I fear."

I wanted to say that she was a lost art, but this was Beverly Hills and who knew what kind of trouble I might be starting so I thanked her and followed Charles to the car.

I visited Pamela Hudson a week later in a medical facility for actors. I found her on a patio dressed in a bathrobe over her pajamas sitting in the sun. She looked like death warmed over — gaunt and jaundiced. I gave her my usual spiel about working at San Simeon and talking to people about their experiences there. She brightened up considerably.

"I'm Marion Davies' niece," she said. "Aunt Marion invited me to visit her at San Simeon to learn about the movie business. It was a wonderful place, so exciting for a girl fresh from the farm." On and on she went about how much she liked it.

I assured her San Simeon was still exciting

even without all the glitter of movie stars.

It took a while, but I finally got her to talk about that specific weekend. "Oh yes, I remember. That was the weekend when I first arrived."

Then I asked her if she remembered Edward Brown.

"Yes." She stopped for a minute, her eyes clouded. "He was the nicest person that I met at San Simeon. Maybe even the nicest person I've met in California. We had a wonderful time on the train going to San Luis Obispo and the next day. We walked around the grounds, saw the Roman Pool, and talked with the movie people. They were all so nice although they had their peculiarities like Arthur Whittingham's crush on Barbara Stanwyck."

She seemed so happy. "Then he left. Without even saying goodbye. I was so mad I cried. Then I heard he was killed and I cried because I was so sad." More than that she didn't know.

I noticed she was wearing a necklace with a small letter B on it. "What's the B for?" I asked.

She giggled and for a moment sounded like the giddy young woman from that weekend so long ago. "It's my initial. I changed my name to Pamela Hudson for the movies. My real name is Becky Stafford."

Not her name, that's what Uncle Edward had said. "Did Edward Brown know."

"Yes." She smiled. "He was so nice to me on the trip up from Los Angeles. He talked to me on the train when nobody else would and gave me his coat when I was cold so I told him my real name. It was all I had to give to him. It was our secret."

I said my goodbyes. I finished with, "I hope you feel better."

She shook her head. "Pancreatic cancer. I won't last another month." Her eyes filled with tears. I beat a hasty, embarrassed retreat.

"Pamela Hudson," I said to Uncle Edward the next time I saw him.

"Not her name," he said back.

"No, it's not. Her name is Becky Stafford."

The pale orb flushed a bright orange. "Yes." Then the orb flushed again and faded away.

Chapter 20

Jack invited me on a picnic with his sister Loraine and her fiancé Mark Mathews. I wasn't sure what motivated the invitation ... did he think he was vetting me with the family? He insisted that the invitation was his sister's idea ... maybe she was vetting me. I'd only met her once briefly last fall. I didn't have anything else to do and the prospect of a picnic on a mountain sounded good. I went to church early on Sunday and quickly changed into a three-quarter length sleeved blouse and Capri pants, jeans with tight fitting legs that stopped at mid-calf. A band through my hair completed my official picnic outfit. Mrs. Rogers gave me a bowl of potato salad fitted inside a canvas bag of ice for the picnic. "You can't let food made with mayonnaise get warm," she warned. "It could poison you." *Then why did you make potato salad for me to bring to a picnic?* I thought, but I couldn't be cross with her. She was really a lovely person and it was a lovely day.

Loraine was a pretty, perky girl about a year older than me. Mark was a couple of years older still. We drove up into the foothills in his four door Ford, Mark and Lorraine sitting close in the front and Jack and I sitting on opposite sides of the seat in the back. He wanted me to move closer. I stayed next to the door. He could have moved over next to me, but that meant he would have to straddle the hump in the floor for the drive shaft and my brother long ago told me no real man would do that. We chatted about this and that until we came to a pull off, then grabbed blankets and picnic baskets to climb the hill.

Once at the top, Loraine and I set about placing the blankets and emptying the picnic basket while the boys, and they were acting just like boys teasing and chasing each other, went back down for the heavy cooler and the charcoal. Mark insisted on cooking on charcoal arranged just so in the stone fire ring. Loraine watched them go down the hill and shook her head. "I'm so glad you could come. Jack wouldn't come without you and he is so good for Mark."

"They look like a couple of ten year olds to

me," I said.

"Mark is usually so serious. He served in the army for six years. Three years in Korea and three years in Germany. Army Corps of Engineers. He loved the work, but as he says, in Korea he never knew when a million Chinese would come after them and in Germany when a million Russians would attack. He didn't like the uncertainty, the waiting. So when his enlistment ran out, he left."

"Oh, well Jack is a good one for bringing out the little boy."

"Yes. Jack says you have been going out for a couple of months now."

I didn't want to go there so I changed the subject. "When are you and Mark going to get married? Jack says that you haven't set a date yet."

"Mark has six more months to go in his probationary period as an Assistant Engineer for the power company. He wants to wait until then when his future with the company is more secure. He's so serious."

Mark and Jack were chasing each other around in a circle with the ice chest in between them. "Not serious now," I observed. Loraine and I giggled.

After a huge picnic lunch to dinner ... it was that big and it was cooking for that long ... Mark settled down on the blanket with his head in Loraine's lap. Jack said, "Who wants to go around the back side of the hill?" Mark and Loraine were looking into each other's eyes pointedly ignoring the suggestion so I said that I would. I had to do something to work off all that food.

"OK," Jack said and we started down a trail. Just before a bend, Jack stopped and told me to close my eyes. "I'll lead you. Don't worry."

He walked me about twenty feet during which time I tripped on a rock, losing my balance and nearly taking him down with me. I was about to put an end to the blindman's walk when he said, "Open your eyes."

The afternoon sun on the castle reflected off the tiles, the bells in their towers, and the outdoor pool. Set up on the hill with the Santa Lucia Mountains as a backdrop, the effect was mystical. "Wow," I said. "Now I understand why Hearst called it the enchanted hill." We sat on a wide, flat rock that seemed to have been intended as a bench and stared.

"Big Jack told me that once, when he was real young, he camped here overnight." Jack indicated an old fire ring in a nearby clearing with a nod of his head. "The castle was really neat at night, all lit up and people walking around. There was music and dancing around the pool and on the terrace. The next morning when he woke up, fog filled the valley. The top of the hill with the castle stuck out in the morning sun. He said it was magical."

A breeze came up making me shiver.

"Cold," Jack asked and put a warm arm around my shoulder. I leaned into him, tilting my head to where it just touched his chest. We sat that way for a minute when Jack leaned down and kissed me, gently, square on the lips. I was surprised, but not displeased. I let him.

"Umm," I said contentedly when he pulled away and I snuggled a little closer. The sun was behind us so we were in the shadow of the hill and he was nice and warm. He bent down and kissed me again a bit more confidently this time. His hand went through my hair and along my neck. He rubbed the back of my neck and my shoulders and moved down my front. I pushed him away. It may have been a while since I'd been kissed, but I wasn't going to tolerate any of that. Jack tried again and this time I slapped his hand away.

"We aren't being very good company," I said and stood. "Let's go back to Lorraine and Mark."

As we rounded the bend in the trail near our picnic spot, Jack came to an abrupt halt. "What ... ?" he said.

I looked past him. It took a second to take in the scene. Mark was lying on the blanket, his pants around his ankles. Loraine was straddling him, her pants with her white panties balled up inside them looking like she'd taken them both off together lying nearby. Her eyes closed, her face contorted, she thrust her pelvis into him. Mark, also with closed eyes met her thrust by thrust. The breeze, blowing from them towards us, carried the sounds she made — something between a growl and a moan — and kept them from hearing Jack's sputtering attempts at speech.

"Come on, let's get out of here before they see us," I said as I grabbed Jack's arm and pulled him back down the trail.

"My sister ..." Jack said not able to compose any more of the sentence.

"No Jack." I spun around to face him. "That was Lorraine and her fiancé. They're engaged to be married. They would already be married from what she told me if he had more faith in his job. She is moving from your family to her own. It's life. Surely you've seen it among your relatives?"

"But ... but ... she. I thought women didn't like that stuff."

I sighed. After our little wrestling match, the ice over this subject seemed thin. "I've never been in love Jack. I understand that a woman in love desires and enjoys physical love as much as a man."

He looked at me and quickly looked away. "So you've never ..."

"No," I said sharper than I intended. "I've never been in love. When that happens, who knows. All people are different." I had a quick mental picture of Dr. Lowe that I suppressed with a shudder. If I was on thin ice now, that direction was positively a whirlpool.

We waited in silence for about ten minutes then worked our way back to the picnic spot talking loudly the last part of the way. Lorraine and Mark, flushed and animated, were packing things up. "How was the view?" Mark asked. "I hear it's great when the sun is on the castle."

Mark and Jack piled the heavy stuff on the cooler and started down the hill. "What's with Jack?" Lorraine said. "He seems a little quiet. You guys didn't have a fight or something, did you?" She picked up the blanket and gave me an end to help her fold it.

"No, we had a spectacular view of the castle," I said thinking. I needed to tell her what Jack had seen. She was his older sister. She would know how to defuse the situation. "It wasn't better than sex."

She stopped in mid fold. "Ah. Did Jack see?"

"Yes and he was a little shaken up by it. I thought you should know before he said something at the wrong time or to the wrong person."

She grimaced. "Thanks. Jack doesn't know as much as he'd like to think. He doesn't spend much time with girls. I'm pretty sure he never got 'the talk' from Dad. When Dad talks to Jack, it's why don't you go to college? Why don't you get a good job? Why do you spend all your time surfing like a bum? I'm afraid he and Mom aren't the greatest role models."

We finished folding the blanket together. When she took it from my hands, she hugged me and said, "Thanks." Then we walked down the hill together to the boys.

Chapter 21

"Mrs. Rogers, have you ever heard of a 'Chinese Theater' in Los Angeles?" I asked in the kitchen after dinner.

"You must mean Grauman's Chinese Theater. That's where all the movie stars have their names and handprints out in the sidewalk. Arthur and I have seen them, but we never went inside to see a movie. That's what it is, a movie theater. Very posh I hear, very expensive."

I was disappointed. "Oh, I thought it might be a venue for Chinese plays or shows — like acrobatics."

"No, just movies. Why do you ask?"

Distracted, I said, "Jack asked me if I wanted to go."

"My, you will be stuck in Los Angeles. The movie will end late and the next train won't leave until dawn."

"We will stay overnight," I said, then put my hands up and shook my head at Mrs. Rogers's shocked look. "April's aunt and uncle invited April and her fiancé Joe as an engagement present. They told her to invite another couple. She told Jack to invite me. We will stay at their house."

Mrs. Rogers seemed to relax.

"A movie theater," I mused. "I wonder why nobody said what movie is showing. Maybe it's a foreign film that nobody has heard of."

Mrs. Rogers said, "Oh, not one where everybody takes their clothes off I hope."

April, Joe, and Jack picked me up in Joe's car. Jack had volunteered to pick everyone up, but we all knew what his car looked like and we vetoed it. Mrs. Rogers handed me half of our lunch to eat on the trip. She had talked to April's mother to coordinate lunch she said. I had a hunch she was vetting the sleeping arrangement and other proprieties. I was looking forward to the trip so much that I couldn't get annoyed.

April's aunt and uncle met us at the station. Mr. and Mrs. Reardon, Aunt Beth and Uncle Chas as they insisted we call them, drove us straight to their house in, as they described it, "the shadow of the Beverly Hills." Aunt Beth marched the girls into a large bedroom with an enormous bathroom. There we primped and preened using the double sinks and mirrored wall in the bath as well as the mirrored vanity table in the bedroom. After the car rides and train ride, we needed some repair. Aunt Beth was a pretty good cosmetologist and the results were near spectacular.

Uncle Chas rapped on the door and said, "Come on girls, time to get a move on."

We followed Aunt Beth out like ducklings swimming along after mama duck. Jack and Joe went from exasperated to open mouthed surprise. Beth had primped me up nicely, but April had gotten a major rework. She kept her eyes down, unable to meet Joe's appreciative stare.

We went to dinner at an elegant French restaurant, La Poubelle Bistro. Chas guided April and Joe through the menu. I said to Jack, "I bet you'd like the Boeff Bourguinon."

Aunt Beth raised her eyes from her menu and gave me a brief wink.

"You should try the Tarteflette Cathy," Uncle Chas said. "It's the best I've ever had."

Chas was a take-charge guy, ordering for all of

us thereby saving the waiter from our brutal attempt at the proper pronunciation. "Where did you learn French?" I asked him.

"The army needed French speakers during the war. I never said so much as 'uh-la-la' in boot camp, but I was ordered to Army French School. I got to 'gay Paree', met Ike, met de Gaulle, ate a lot of French food. Now I'm in publicity and use my training to order at French restaurants."

After dinner we drove a few blocks and into a gated parking lot behind a building. "Sorry, we have to sneak in the back door," Chas said.

We went into a well-lit door and up the elevator. Getting out, we took the first side corridor and from the window, we looked out over the street. The entrance to the building was brightly, almost harshly lit. A long, black car pulled up, a uniformed doorman opened the back door, and a formally dressed couple emerged. They smiled and waved to the crowd as they walked up the red carpet, flashbulbs punctuating their every move.

"Tonight's the West Coast opening of *Teacher's Pet*. The show starts in 15 minutes ... we should get to our seats."

An usher took our tickets and escorted us to

our seats. They reminded me of the seats in the upper deck at Yankee Stadium. Everyone there seemed to be connected to the movie industry and was dressed to kill.

The movie was a nice comedy, not too deep with a lot of good laughs. It starred Clark Gable, Doris Day, and Mamie Van Doren. Of course, the polar opposites got together at the end with the promise of living happily every after.

After the credits, we filed out with the rest of the audience, but we broke away from the crowd to a door attended by a pair of ushers. After a quick word with Chas and a nose count of our party, we were in.

We walked into a party of the Hollywood beautiful and powerful. I didn't recognize anyone. I could tell that I was out of my depth. Even Chas, who had been Mr. Suave and Confident all evening looked on edge. I watched as he scanned the room, found who he was looking for, and gave a small wave.

I followed his gaze and froze. Clark Gable detached himself from a group and walked our way. As he passed Doris Day, who was talking to a gray haired woman in a stunning blue gown, he tapped Doris on the shoulder and whispered. Together, they walked to our little group.

"Doris, Clark. So happy you could take a minute to talk to us. You know my wife Beth," Chas said. There were smiles and nods. "And this is my niece April and her fiancé Joe."

Doris reached over and took April by both hands, then kissed her on the cheek. "Best wishes for a life together filled with happiness," Doris whispered.

Clark pumped Joe's hand. "You are one lucky guy. Congratulations.

The next moment would have been awkward for mere mortals, but it was apparently a basic maneuver in the Hollywood Stars Playbook. Doris took Joe's hand and repeated her wish for their happiness. Clark kissed April on the cheek and repeated Joe was a lucky guy. The entire maneuver was smooth and natural. Chas then introduced us as her friends.

Doris asked April about the wedding plans, which started an animated conversation. I wasn't listening. Clark Gable had been at San Simeon that weekend.

I touched his sleeve. "Mr. Gable. My uncle told me he met you once a long time ago, at San Simeon."

"I visited there many times. What's you uncle's name."

"Edward Brown. He worked for Mr. Hearst."

Gable furrowed his brow. "Hmmm. I can't say as I remember him."

I didn't know how he would take it, but I had to try. "He said that when he met you, you were in your underwear."

His brow unfurrowed, his face morphed into a grin. "'Mr. Edward Brown, employee of Mr. Hearst.' I remember. We both had rooms in the guesthouse that overlooks the ocean. The moon was nearly full so I stayed up to watch it set. I was in my underwear so I could jump right into bed afterward. His car was very late. He came into the sitting room where we met. Nice guy."

Oh Uncle Edward. You're turning me into a believer.

We came back to Beth and Chas' house after the party. They brought us into what they called the Family Room and lit a gas fireplace. I'd never seen one of them before. Then Chas opened a bottle of champagne.

"To April and Joe. May they have a long and happy married life together ... and lots and lots of children."

April blushed as we raised our glasses and drank to them. Chas refilled our four glasses again and said, "The old folks need to go to bed. Bedrooms are upstairs ... boys to the left, girls to the right."

We sat and talked in low tones, sipping our champagne. When I finished my glass, I got up to go upstairs, giving Jack a little tug to follow. As we climbed the stairs, I heard April and Joe whispering, then she giggled and they were quiet.

At the top of the stairs, Jack started to speak. I spun to face him. "Shhhh. They're engaged. Let them have a little quiet time alone together," I said.

He nodded and smiled, hooking his arms around my waist. "Did you enjoy today?" he whispered.

"Wow, did I ever!" I said as the events of the day came flooding back. Exuberant, I put my arms around his neck. He put his lips on mine and kissed me and ... I kissed him back.

April came into our room a few minutes later a little flushed. I was sitting on the edge of one of the beds, clutching my pajamas to my chest.

"Cathy, are you all right?"

"I kissed him. A real kiss. I was so excited about today, it just got away from me. Now Jack is going to think I'm leading him on." My mood had deflated from just a few minutes ago.

"Are your sure you didn't mean it?" April had an innuendo in her voice. I ignored it.

"Now what am I going to do?"

Chapter 22

Carefully I negotiated the big, black car through the winding streets. The development wasn't large, but the houses were on large lots, the windy streets designed to give the area "interest." It was a far cry from the small houses on cramped lots that dotted much of the state.

The car, a 1957 Cadillac, was bigger than anything I had ever driven. Even Mom's 1955 Buick was modest by comparison. I thought that my Nash would make a fine spare car. It could fit into the trunk. I worried about the extra size so I drove slow and gave the turns a wide berth. Any cop who saw me would assume I was drunk which I assuredly was not. A Champagne toast and one glass of Pinot with dinner did not make me the slightest bit tipsy. I had discovered what it took to make me drunk at Mary Streeter's party my sophomore year. I also discovered what a hangover was all about, an experience that I didn't want to repeat.

Jack, sitting on the passenger side of the front seat, was drunk. He'd started drinking highballs during the cocktail hour and kept up a steady intake of alcohol all the way through dinner. He didn't argue when I said I would drive home, but he slid across the front seat to sit close to me. I slapped him away. When he persisted I pulled to the side of the road and told him I would toss the keys into the sewer unless he behaved. Now he sulked, huddled against the passenger's door, occasionally giving me cryptic directions.

"Turn left."

"Next right."

"Number seven."

Jack gave a muted groan as I meandered down the dark street trying to read the house numbers by the glow of the anemic porch lights. I spotted a seventy-two ... we were at the far end of the street. I sped up.

"Stop," Jack said, more a plea than an order.

"We aren't near ..."

"Please ... stop." I pulled to the curb and stopped. He opened the door, hung his head out, and retched. I'd seen my brother get sick once after drinking too much. He vomited with a violence that gave the impression he was proud of it. Not Jack. He sounded more like a gurgly whimper. The smell of whiskey and partially digested beef wafted into the car. I cranked the window open furiously.

One car passed us from the front and, a minute later, another from the rear. Jack puked some more. After he had been quiet for a minute, I went into my purse and found a hankie, one of the rose patterned ones that my Grandmother had given me for Christmas three years ago. I brushed the hankie against Jack's hand, the one clutching the dashboard. He was twisted around with his head out the door, the other hand supporting his weight so that he didn't go headlong into the gutter and ... I decided not to complete that thought. He pulled himself up and took the hankie. "Thanks," he managed to say weakly.

Once in the driveway of Jack's home, he got out of the car and went straight into the house not bothering to shut the front door behind him. I followed cautiously dangling the car keys from my hand. Jack's father, convinced that I was sober and I had driven the car home without incident, called a cab for me. Then he headed up the stairs saying, "I have to talk to my son." Poor Jack.

Jack's mother came down and apologized, She also gave me an appraising look. We walked out onto the porch. "Don't think too badly of Jack," she said. "He doesn't ..." She couldn't quite find the words to complete the thought. I told her that it was all right, things happen, and so on. I don't remember all that I said. She nodded. "I'm beginning to understand what Jack sees in you," she said.

Lorraine came out and gave me a hug. "Are you OK?"

I assured her that I was.

"Dad's furious with Jack. I think he is angry about what could have happened to his car first and what other people in town are going to think of him second. Worrying about Jack comes near dead last and I'm afraid you don't even make the list."

"That's sad," I said thinking of my Dad.

"Jack's taken with you. Did you know he is going back to college in the fall? He didn't want to tell you until he had picked out all his courses. He wanted to impress you."

I didn't know what to think about that.

She stayed with me until the taxi came.

"He's still a little kid in a lot of ways," Lorraine

said.

We said our goodbyes and I got into the cab.

Mr. and Mrs. Rogers were waiting for me. They knew April's grandparents so they wanted to know all about the wedding. I told them, leaving out the part about Jack, but they had noticed I came home in a cab so the story came out. Jack lost quite a few points in their estimation. That is if he ever had any points to begin with.

Well, I thought to myself as I finally slipped under the covers. I'll remember April's wedding. She looked so happy. Jack looked so miserable.

Chapter 23

The names on my list were being relentlessly eliminated. Despite the 20 years since that weekend in San Simeon, I located quite a number of the people on the list and talked with them. Several others had died and a couple were A List movie stars who wouldn't talk to a mere mortal such as me. Meeting Clark Gable was a stroke of luck unlikely to be repeated.

Pamela Hudson, actually Becky Stafford, provided the most information, but nothing helpful in identifying Edward's killer or when and where he had actually been killed. Two more names remained — Bruce Schwartz and Arthur Whittingham. I went to the Los Angeles library to read their bio files.

I found Arthur Whittingham first or, to be precise, I found his obituary. He'd died in 1937 only a few weeks after Edward. I sighed and closed the file.

My stomach informed me by way of an unladylike rumble that it was lunchtime. I went into the park across the street and sat on an unoccupied bench under a tree. I unpacked the sandwich that I'd made that morning. A sidelong glance from a passing young executive type alerted me that I might not be alone for long, such was my experience with the outgoing young men of downtown LA. I was irritable, not in the mood to make new friends so I opened a newspaper that was left on the bench. Yesterdays. No matter. I didn't have the time or the interest to read much. It was opened to the news of the movie industry. Of course. This was LA where the movie industry was a major occupation and preoccupation.

Thus hidden I picked a story and started to read. I read through my cheese sandwich and half an apple. I stopped in mid-bite when I read at the end of the article, "The new film is being produced by Bruce Schwartz in conjunction with RKO studios."

A phone call to RKO got me in touch with his secretary. I'd found that the simple half-truth, "I'm involved with the opening of San Simeon and I'd like to discuss his recollections of visiting there..." opened many doors. I made an appointment for a meeting for next Tuesday just after lunch.

I had no vacation and no more sick days. Still, Dr. Lowe didn't seem concerned that I would be out on Tuesday. I was too excited about seeing Bruce Schwartz to care why. I arrived for the meeting just before 1 P.M. and waited. I discovered that after lunchtime was probably the least desirable time for an appointment since a movie executive's lunch could stretch well into the afternoon. I hoped that Schwartz wouldn't be drunk as well as late. About quarter after two I heard a nearby door open and close and a minute later the secretary showed me into the inner office.

My heart sunk when I saw him. He was only a few years older than me. He couldn't be the Bruce Schwartz from the weekend. Well, I'd played hooky from work and come all this way so I launched into my spiel. I started by slightly misrepresenting myself and my role at San Simeon to get him talking about his experiences at the castle and planned to segue into that weekend.

That turned out to be easier than expected. Bruce Schwartz the elder had taken his son to San Simeon on day trips several times while working with Hearst. The older Schwartz would meet with Hearst while the boy roamed the grounds, the wild animal cages being a favorite destination.

About five minutes into the meeting, the secretary discretely popped in and left an envelope on the desk. "Personal to you from the head of the studio," she said and withdrew. I feared that Schwartz would end the interview, saying he had to attend to the letter immediately. Not a problem. He continued to roll down memory lane. I sat back taking a few notes and looking attentive and pretty. I'd discovered looking attentive and pretty could get a man to talk and talk and talk. I waited for him to wind down.

When he seemed about finished, I said, "There was a particular party on August 29, 1936. Your father was on the guest list. Do you remember your father talking about it at all?"

"No, I'm sorry, but I don't. Is it important?"

"My uncle was at the party also. I'm trying to find out what I can about that weekend. You see, my uncle was found murdered the next day..."

Schwartz slammed his fist down on the desk. "So that's your game," he yelled. His face turned red, a vein stood out on his temple. The transformation took my breath away. "You're trying to pin your uncle's death on my father. Why not? He killed Whittingham. Why not your uncle?"

"What? He killed Arthur Whittingham?" That hadn't been in the obituary.

"Oh sure, like you didn't know. We're finished here." He picked up the envelope and opened the middle drawer of his desk. The secretary appeared silently at my side. He glanced up and said, "She's leaving." The secretary put her hand on my shoulder. Schwartz slit open the envelope.

I rose halfway out of the chair and froze. "Do you know what that is?" I said.

"It's a god-damn letter from the head of the god-damn studio!"

"No, the opener."

It lay on the desk. The handle was carved silver. The blade curved.

Schwartz stared at it with new eyes. "No. It belonged to my father."

"It's a sixteenth century Persian dress dagger from the Hearst collection."

He stared at the dagger some more, then pushed it toward me. "Here. Take it and leave."

There would be formalities of course. The dagger would have to be authenticated by an expert and identified as belonging to the Hearst collection. A letter thanking Bruce Schwartz for restoring a valuable artifact to the collection would be written and sent. Schwartz might even get a charitable deduction on his income tax. I had another stop to make first.

John Brady was taking a nap, so his wife said, but he came into the room while we were speaking. "Hi, I thought I recognized the voice."

I unwrapped the dagger and laid it on the table. "What do you think?"

He got out a ruler and measured the dagger, both the length and curve of the blade. "It matches the description in the coroner's report. He eyed me. "Where did you get it?"

"Off the record?"

He chuckled without mirth. "Technically, no murder case is closed until there is a conviction, but the only people who care about this one are in this room."

So I told him. About Becky. About Arthur Whittingham and Barbara Stanwyck. About the Bruce Schwartzes, father and son. He stood silent for long time, then he nodded.

"Yes. I remember the Whittingham murder. Schwartz and Whittingham hated each other for years. We suspected that your uncle's murder might have taken place at the Castle. The powers that be thought it such a long shot that they didn't want to bother Hearst. They worried that he might turn his newspapers against us. And it wasn't like we didn't have enough work to do."

Chapter 24

I walked the path to the Roman Pool. The day was magic. The blue sky painted lightly with mare's tails met a Pacific Ocean capped with white foam. Bird songs shrill and boisterous competed with the buzzing bass of insects. A ground squirrel sped by me without so much as a by your leave. Expectation charged the air like an approaching Midwest lightening storm.

In the Roman Pool the elements were subdued save for the sunlight tearing through the tall windows, albeit mellowed by the amber glass, sending reflections of the water dancing on the ceiling and setting the tiles aglow. I slipped off my shoes not wishing to have the clicking of my heels on the tile floor disturb the serenity of the scene. The humid air warmed my skin.

Automatically I smoothed my hair as if Edward

could notice. I reverently walked around to the diving area away from the bright sunlight. There, in this spot illuminated by the diffuse light of the pool water, I sat cross-legged and whispered, "Uncle Edward. It's Cathy. I'm here."

A small ripple fluttered on the surface of the pool. A dim light reluctantly appeared. The moist air took on a chill. I knew that this was going to be our last meeting. I'd fulfilled my promise. The castle would open to the public soon. I think he sensed this as well.

"Uncle Edward, I know who killed you. It was a mistake. The note wasn't meant for you. It was meant to lure someone else to the pool that night. I'm so sorry."

A huge, mournful sigh washed over my body. I crossed my hands over my chest and hunched my shoulders against the chill. "Thank you Cathy, dear child. It's so good of you to do this for me." The words appeared in my head wrapped in melancholy.

"Uncle Edward. I found her. Becky. Becky Stafford. She remembers you. She said you were the nicest person she ever met. She was angry with you when she found out you had gone the morning after the costume party. When she found out you ... died, she cried. She said she still misses you."

The glow over the pool brightened a bit and changed color. A warmth suffused my body.

Voices filtered in from outside. They weren't coming in here I knew. It was past five o-clock. People were leaving for the day. I should too.

"I have to leave now Uncle Edward," I said. "I don't know when ... if I can come back."

"I know." Understanding and warmth filled me. "Be well. Thank you again so very much." Edward faded away.

I joined the workers heading towards the parking lot. Phoebe fell into step along side me. "Cathy," she said, concern in her voice, "are you crying?"

Chapter 25

Adam called just as I got in from work. Mrs. Rogers handed me the phone saying, "It's that nice Mr. Spencer." I don't remember him being "that nice Mr. Spencer" before. He must be growing on her.

"Can you meet me at our place for dinner," he said. "There are developments in the case you'll want to hear about."

After he'd hung up, I realized he'd called it "our place" as if we were secret lovers. I made my apologies to Mrs. Rogers, who didn't seem bothered that I skipped out on dinner at the last minute, and went upstairs to dress. I put on the blue polka-dot dress, the one I'd worn the first night we'd met at the Mountain Roost and we'd seen Lowe in the parking lot. I didn't think much about it — only that it was comfortable, looked nice, and went well with the white sweater I'd bought last week in LA. The days were warmer, but the nights still chilly.

Adam was already at Andre's when I arrived, sitting at the table in an alcove. As I walked to the table the owner gave me a smile and a wave. A woman with gray hair, half of a couple who were regulars, saw me and nudged her husband. He looked up as I passed by. They exchanged a knowing look. We were getting a reputation.

A bottle of Pinot stood in an ice bucket next to the table. After I took off my sweater and sat down, Adam, looking pleased, said, "We arrested Lowe." Now I knew why he'd ordered the wine for us to share rather than his usual beer and my glass of house white. He wanted to tell me more, but the waiter appeared in an instant to take our orders. "The trout almondine is very good tonight," he said.

Adam told me the story. "Lowe and Pieter ran a cute scam. Lowe would take the paintings from the warehouse. Pieter would copy them. Pieter learned his forgery technique from Han van Meegeren ..."

"Van Meegeren? The man who forged Vermeer?" Van Meegeren, a legend among art forgers, specialized in paintings by the Dutch Master Vermeer. During World War II, Nazi bigwig Herman Goering unknowingly bought one of his forgeries.

After the war, the Dutch government traced the sale of the painting back to van Meegeren and charged him with collaboration, a crime punishable by death. He admitted to forgery to avoid execution. If he hadn't confessed, his forgeries might still pass as genuine.

"I'm impressed," Adam said. "Do they teach art crime in college?"

"Forgery is a part of art history. But the painting that had the fresh oil paint on the frame was a watercolor," I said.

"Right. A buyer appeared who really loved that water color. Lowe couldn't pass up the money. Pieter must have been a little careless. We figure he put the watercolor in the same easel he'd also used for an oil. You know how long oil paint takes to dry, especially if it's right out of the tube and hasn't been thinned."

"Yes." I scooped up a bit more of the trout almondine. It was delicious. "Still, I'm sure all the paintings I examined were originals. I'm not an expert, but I've had some experience in Boston and New York. Was Pieter that good?"

"Yes, Pieter's that good, but that's not the best part. Lowe sold the forgeries and returned the originals to the warehouse. He sold to people who had more money than art sense. They weren't likely to notice a forgery." Adam grinned. "What could Lowe's customers do if they found out? Not go to the police. If they confronted Lowe, he would return the money and take the painting back claiming he'd been fooled. Since the buyers didn't know each other, they weren't likely to alert one another. Lowe planned on leaving with Pieter and the money next month. That's one reason he was so slow in examining all the paintings in the warehouse. He didn't want any of them on exhibit until after he left the country. What a scheme."

"How did you ever catch them?"

He smiled. "When you identified Pieter, we wondered how he fit into the puzzle. Then one of the buyers bragged about the painting he just bought to a friend. He didn't know that the friend knew the Governor. The Governor sent him to us and we discovered the painting was a fake. We set up a sting. Lowe didn't recognize me. I guess our play acting in the parking lot at the Mountain Roost worked."

He picked up his wine glass to drink. I picked up mine and we touched them together. "Good job detective," I said. Then an unsettling thought came. "Will there be a trial? Will I have to testify? In court?"

Adam's smile turned into a thin line, his face narrowed.

"Too many of the buyers are well connected in Sacramento, to the Governor or other politicians. They would have to testify if the case went to trial, which would be embarrassing to them. The ADA, that's the Assistant District Attorney, made a deal with Lowe and Pieter. The forged paintings were confiscated as evidence, the money returned to the extent possible — Lowe managed to spend a bit already — and Lowe and Pieter will cop a plea to Larceny. Not even Grand Larceny! They may spend some time in jail, but probably not. The ADA doesn't want them teaching Art Appreciation to the inmates at San Quentin."

"They aren't dangerous, are they?" The memory of Pieter's grip came back to me with a chill. Goosebumps popped up on my bare arms.

Adam seemed to understand. "Pieter will be deported to the Netherlands once the State of California finishes with him. Lowe will probably go with him if the Dutch government overlooks his record. Neither of them knows about your involvement. They think we suspected them because of a tip from the Ferus Gallery. That's true, just not the whole truth, so we let them believe it."

"I'm sorry," I said and I was. Adam had worked

hard on this case. "You deserve more credit."

The smile crept back, a little rueful. "Oh, I'll come out all right. A lot of people owe people favors to fix things up. It works out. Not the way they teach you in law school, but it works out."

"The forged paintings are kept as evidence?"

He nodded.

"Pity, I really liked that watercolor."

"I'll talk to the ADA. People owe people favors, remember. Sometimes evidence disappears. Maybe not real soon, but sometimes."

After the waiter set down the dessert and coffee, I said, "I've finished my investigation into my uncle's murder. I know who killed him." I told him the story just as I'd told it to Brady. Adam listened intent, asking questions.

"You'd never get to court with that story, but it's plausible. I'm surprised you came up with plausible after all this time. Did you tell Brady?"

"Yes. He measured the dagger and said it matched the autopsy report. He said it was a good as we were likely to get."

Adam nodded his agreement.

Adam paid for dinner and we got up to leave. He helped me with my sweater. As we walked out to the parking lot, Adam said, "Well, I guess this is our last dinner." It was just a statement. There was no emotion in his voice.

In the excitement, I hadn't realized. Unbidden, words came to my lips, "There's Lowe. Quick, pretend to kiss me."

"Huh," he said and stopped. I spun around in front of him, one arm up around his neck. I pulled him down and to me and took off his hat with my other hand. I put my lips on his. He tasted of steak and Pinot and smelled of after-shave. He'd shaved for our dinner! He put his arms around my waist and lifted me into him. Our lips parted. I melted into him. He felt so good.

Epilogue

Epilogue

Cambria, California

June 18, 1960

I looked at the bride in the mirror and made a face. She made one back. *Damn, where was everybody?* My mother left with the photographer a few minutes ago after the obligatory "Mom straightening the veil" pictures. For a minute I was happy to be alone but ... it was too close to the ceremony to be abandoned. April went to the Ladies Room for the fourth time. Mary Claire and Clarissa went for a smoke. Here I am ... alone.

"I'm back," April said as she navigated into the room.

April was my Matron of Honor. She was very pregnant. Still she swore she wasn't due for two more weeks and a day and she hadn't felt a contraction yet. She glowed like she had swallowed a light bulb. What a contrast to the April of two years ago. That April, newly engaged, was nervous and shy. The girls who'd known her since grade school said that marriage was good for her. It brought the old April back, only better. Joe was the man. They completed each other.

"I hope you don't have to go in the middle of the ceremony," I said.

"Naw, don't worry. It's just the baby on my bladder."

The fabric stretched tight across her belly undulated. She rubbed the spot. "He doesn't want to miss a minute of your big day."

Mary Claire and Clarissa flew into the room like a pair of pink chiffon crows and cackled with raucous laughter.

"Guess who we saw," Clarissa said. "Jack Goode and his *date*. She has hair down to her butt and is dressed like a gypsy."

"Jack's father looks like a volcano about to pop his cork," Mary Claire said. "Daddy got his wish ... Jack went back to college, but he doesn't look happy with the girl he brought home."

April said, "Cathy, I'm sorry I tried to push you and Jack together. You're not mad at me, are you?"

I stretched over the expanse of April's

midsection and kissed her cheek, lightly so as not to muss her makeup or my lipstick.

"Oh don't be silly. He was cute and someone to be with. That's all."

A tap at the door. "Is everybody decent in there?" said my father.

"Oh Bill, you're too much. Of course they're decent." My mother pushed open the door. She wore powder blue, her favorite color. The color that made her eyes stand out. Bewitching eyes my father called them.

"Gawd, I feel like I'm caught in the hen house," he said, "with a lovely flock of hens." My family had come in from Iowa on the train three days ago. Mary Claire, Clarissa, and April lined up to peck my father on the cheek. They all loved him.

Mom blew an exasperated sigh. "Don't play farmer today Bill. You never were a good farmer."

A rap on the door. My brother Bud stuck in his head. "Mom, it's time. The organist ran out of church music and played 'Take Me Out to the Ball Game.'" He grinned.

"Your mother made me wait forty minutes at the altar," Dad said.

Bud rolled his eyes.

Mom got up and Bud let her out the door. He looked back and said, "You look great Sis."

A compliment from my big brother. Already this was a day to remember.

We started down the aisle. Adam waited for me at the altar. A mental fog blew in. The ceremony came to me in bits through the fog.

Dad put my hand into Adam's. "Take good care of her, son," he said and was gone.

We stood. We sat. We knelt.

Adam looked into my eyes and spoke.

I spoke. "For better or for worse, for richer or for poorer, til death do us part."

Father Antonio said, "You may kiss the bride."

Adam's lips touched mine, a demure kiss as we'd decided beforehand. I could feel hunger behind it.

"W-o-o-o w-o-o-o," said April.

Come on April. It's not that much of a kiss I thought. There was an intake of breath from the pews.

"O-o-w damn, my water broke," said April.

Joe took April to the hospital. At the reception, people waited in shifts at the pay phone for updates. April was fine but, as a legion of mothers and grandmothers told us, first babies take their time.

After the reception, we went to the hospital still
wearing tux and wedding dress.

"She's good," Joe said. "The doctor says it will
take all night. Go on your honeymoon."

"We can't leave while our favorite people are
having a baby," Adam said. Oh God, how I loved this
man.

"You guys are great," Joe said. He handed
Adam his keys. "Stay in the bungalow. I won't be
getting home tonight."

"Still want a baby?" Adam said in the car.

"Oh yes. You?"

His hand closed around mine and squeezed.
"Yes."

Chilled water washed over me. I'd targeted the
wedding for the middle of my cycle so that there
would be no "female" problems on the honeymoon.
Menstrual algebra was not precise. Still ... tonight
could be the night.

Joe and April had bought the tiny bungalow
from his widowed Aunt Trudy. Adam carried me
across the threshold and into the bedroom, put me
down on the bed, and went out for the suitcases. A
double bed. I hadn't been in a double bed since I was
a sick little girl and Mom let me sleep in their bed

during the day. I reached out and felt the vast, empty expanse where Adam would be. Then he was there, kissing me, undoing one-by-one the formation of buttons that ran down the back of my gown. Tomorrow night. I'd wear my new nightgown tomorrow night.

I lay curled up next to Adam, exhilarated, exhausted, sticky, as the rhythm of his breathing lulled me to sleep. *This is the bed where April and Joe conceived their baby* was my last conscious thought.

It was eleven o'clock before we got to the hospital. Joe woke with a start when we tapped the door to April's room.

Joe looked devastated in the remains of his tuxedo.

April looked worse. Puffy, blotchy. But her smile was still there.

"So, tell us the news," I said after a hug and a kiss.

April's eyes got wide. "You don't know? Well, they're bringing the babies out now." The hall filled with nurses.

A nurse came and gave April a blue-blanketed bundle, a pink face with dark hair poked out.

224

"Oh he's beautiful," I said and leaned over April to get a better look.

Adam cleared his throat. I looked up at him and he was wide-eyed and smiling. "Cathy, behind you."

I moved and let a second nurse put a pink-blanketed bundle in April's other arm.

Joe moved to the foot of the bed. "Aunt Trudy warned me. That was the bed where she and Uncle Charlie made their twins, Bart and Johnny. Powerful bed is what she called it. A real twin bed."

Once again the chill washed over me. We'd just last night ... In that same bed! I looked over at Adam. His eyes were glazed. He was pale. He'd stopped smiling.